# *Elisa*

# Elisa

Book Two of the Alpha Series

# E. L. Todd

# 1

"So, she really isn't leaving?" Alex asked.

"No."

He was quiet for a moment. "And you're okay with that?"

I shrugged. "It's her life. I can only advise her to do so much. Besides, they are getting married."

"Are you serious?"

"Yeah."

The sadness was obvious in his eyes. I felt bad for the guy but at the same time I didn't. Sadie had been single forever. He shouldn't have waited until she found a boyfriend to make his move. "I—I didn't know that."

"Yeah."

"Isn't it too soon?"

"I thought so too, but Sadie is intent on it. She's moving in with him and Elisa."

He looked at me. "Have you talked to her?"

I didn't like talking about Elisa. "No."

"I'm sorry, man."

"I'm over it." Nothing could be further from the truth. I was a walking shadow.

"Well, it's better this way anyway. Did you really want to be a stepdad?"

I loved those kids. They were a pain in the ass but they were adorable. I would do anything to be with Elisa. "No."

"See?" he said triumphantly.

I ignored him. "Aren't you glad it didn't work out with Sadie? She's a pain in the ass."

His face fell. "I guess."

I leaned back in my chair and looked around at the women of the bar. A lot of them were beautiful but I had no interest in them. I felt like I was blind to the world around me. It was like someone squeezed lemon juice in my eye and I couldn't see anyone but Elisa because my brain had memorized her face perfectly.

"That girl is cute," Alex said as he stared across the room.

"Eh," I said without looking.

"Come on. Go over there and ask her out."

"I don't want to."

He stared at me. "Just do it, Jared. Get back on the horse."

I sighed. "I'm just not in the mood."

"Get over it and get in the mood."

"Why don't you go hit on someone?"

"I will but I have to make sure you're going first."

I took another drink of my beer. "Fine." I looked at the thin blonde. She had long legs, a flat stomach, and a nice chest. "I'll see you later."

"Good luck," Alex said as he held up his beer.

I walked over to the girl who was sitting alone. She stared at me when I approached her. When she smiled at me, I knew she was interested.

"Hey, I'm Jared. I left my keys over here. Have you seen them?"

She looked at the counter. "I'm sorry. No, I haven't."

"Okay," I said with a sigh. "I have a spare in my apartment. I'll just have the super let me in tomorrow."

She nodded. "Why can't you ask him tonight?"

"He's out for the night. I'll stay in a motel or something."

"You don't have friends in the city?"

"No," I said sadly. "I just moved here and started working on Wall Street. I'm pretty new to this big city."

Her eyes lit up with interest when she heard what I did for a living. It seemed to work on most girls. "Where are you from?"

"Pennsylvania."

"That's cute."

I smiled. "Cute?"

"Don't the Dutch live there?"

"Yes, but I'm not Dutch."

She smiled at me.

"Well, thanks for your help. Have a good night." I turned away but she spoke to me.

"Jared?"

"Yes?" I asked as I came back to her.

"My name is Shelly."

"Oh? I'm so sorry. Where are my manners? It was very nice to meet you, Shelly." I turned away again.

"Would you like to buy me a drink?"

I looked at her. "Sure. Of course I would." I returned to the bar and sat next to her. She turned toward me and smiled at me blatantly. When the bartender came over, she ordered her drink.

"So, how's Wall Street?" she asked.

"Good. I like it."

"Where did you go to school?"

"Harvard."

She smiled. "So, you're super smart?"

"I know a few things," I said humbly.

"You're cute."

"Like the Dutch?"

She laughed. "And you're funny."

I smiled. I had this girl. I was going to get laid tonight if I wanted to. "So, what do you do for a living, Shelly?"

"I work as a model for Macy's."

I took a drink of my beer. "That isn't surprising."

She smiled. "I'll take that as a compliment."

"It was meant as one."

"Are you in New York permanently?"

"I think so."

"Good."

That made her smile wider.

She and I talked for a while. I tried to concentrate on what she was saying but I really wasn't interested. She was nice and beautiful, but I just didn't care. I kept thinking about Elisa, and I wondered what she was doing. I remembered our afternoon trip to the park. The kids were loud and playful but they were also really fun. Elisa's brown hair was so soft. I always wanted to touch it. She was the most beautiful woman I had ever seen. That was the initial reason I was so attracted to her, but after I got to know her, I fell in love with her. She was exceptional. I wish she was ready to move past her husband. I knew she wanted me but she wouldn't let herself have me. She thought it was disrespectful to her husband. I understood and respected her feelings even though I wasn't happy about them.

"And then the pie was everywhere," she said with a laugh.

I started laughing because she started laughing. I had no idea what she said but I just played along.

She placed her hand on mine. "Since you don't have anywhere to stay tonight, do you want to stay at my place?" Her fingers glided across my knuckles.

I said nothing for a moment. I didn't want to sleep around because of Elisa, but since she wasn't going to be with me, I knew I should move on. Maybe if I slept with someone, it might push me forward. "That would be wonderful," I said with a smile. "That's very generous of you."

I paid the bill then we left the bar, heading up the street until a cab pulled over. She placed her hand on my thigh and squeezed then she moved her hand over my crotch, massaging me. I started to get hard at her ministrations. I was definitely going to score with this girl.

When we reached her apartment building, I paid the cab driver then we climbed out and walked into the building. When we were in the elevator, she leaned into me and I wrapped my arm around her waist. The doors opened and we walked to her room. I felt my heart pounding.

I wasn't ready for this. All I could think about was Elisa. Would it hurt her if she knew I slept with someone? I thought it would. She didn't want me but I couldn't do this. The girl stuck her key in the door then opened it. I didn't step through. I stayed outside the door. Guilt flooded through me when I considered sleeping with that girl. I was in love with someone else. I couldn't do it. "I'm sorry," I said as I turned around.

The last thing I saw was her shocked expression before I walked down the hallway toward the elevator. I took the stairway to the left then headed down to the street. Instead of taking a cab, I walked back to my apartment building, thinking about Elisa the whole way. I just had to get over her before I started dating and sleeping with other women. I wasn't sure how possible that would be. My sister was moving in with Ethan and they were getting married. I had a feeling I would be seeing a lot more of Elisa.

# 2

"So, what did you do last night?" Sadie asked from across the table. We were eating breakfast together like we usually did on the weekend.

"Nothing interesting."

"Did you go out with Alex?"

"We went to a bar."

"Did you meet anyone?"

I was quiet for a moment. "No one worth remembering."

She caught my saddened expression. "I'm sorry, Jared."

"It's okay. It's not your fault."

"Do you want me to talk to her?"

"That's the last thing I want. Leave it alone, Sadie. She made her decision and I respect it."

"Maybe she would change her mind if you chased her."

I shook my head. "This isn't a bad breakup she's recovering from. She's a widow—*a widow*. I'm not just going to manipulate her into being with me. It doesn't work like that. She has to come to me."

"But what if she never does?"

"That's her decision to make, Sadie."

She took a drink of her coffee. "What if Ethan talked to her?"

"Drop it."

"I just hate seeing you like this."

"I'll get over it," I said as I ate my waffles. "Let's discuss something else."

"Well, I need to start packing."

"You're not going to fit all your stuff in his townhouse."

She sighed. "I know."

"What are you going to do?"

"Sell my furniture."

"All of it?"

She nodded.

I wanted to tell her that this relationship was moving too fast but I knew she wouldn't listen to me. She was never logical when it came to Ethan. I liked Ethan a lot. I admit I was wrong about him before and I knew he had changed, but I still thought they were moving too quick.

"Spill it."

"What?"

"I know you aren't comfortable with this and you think I should change my mind."

I was quiet for a moment. "It's your life, Sadie."

"I'm happy, Jared, and I know that I'm not making a mistake."

"Then you don't need my approval."

"Yes, I do. You're my brother."

I sighed. "It is too fast, Sadie. I have a bowl of fruit that's been in my refrigerator longer than you and Ethan have been together."

"Ethan and I are different."

"You're just hung up on him because he's the first pretty boy to give you the eye," I snapped.

She glared at me. "I love Ethan for who he is, not just for his looks."

"I'm sorry. I just don't want you to get hurt."

"I won't," she said gently. "And even if it doesn't work out, I still wouldn't change any of this. I want to be with him for as long as I can even if it doesn't last."

I stared at her smile and knew she meant what she said. She really was in love with that guy. Nothing I said would change anything so I knew I should just be supportive. "Then I'm happy for you."

She smiled. "Really?"

"Truly," I said. "But if you don't see me around his place, it's not because of you."

"I understand," she said sadly. "You'll move on eventually."

I hoped she was right but I really doubted it. I had a beautiful woman who wanted me to stay at her place the night before but I said no. I was either madly in love or I was gay.

"So you want to help me pack?"

"Do you want to help clean my bathroom?"

She rolled her eyes. "Those aren't even comparable. I don't think you've cleaned your bathroom once since you moved in."

"And you would be right."

"So, you'll help?"

"Isn't that your fiancé's job?"

"Just because I'm getting married doesn't mean our relationship will ever change, Jared. I'll still need you."

I said nothing. That was another fear that I had, that Ethan would take her away. It was going to happen one day but I didn't expect it to happen so soon.

"Come on. Let's go."

I tossed some cash on the table and we left the restaurant. When we walked inside her apartment, I sighed. "You haven't packed anything."

Koku ran to me and started to paw at my legs.

"Hey, man," I said as I picked him up. "You must be excited to move. Now you'll have two little kids to play with you."

He barked.

I scratched his head. "Good boy." I put him down. "Well, since you aren't bringing any furniture, I guess it won't be so bad. And they probably have all the kitchen supplies."

"Yeah, that's true."

I moved to the couch and sat down, turning on the television. "I'll be here if you need me."

She rolled her eyes. "Thanks for all the help."

"Hey, I'll move your boxes and junk for you, but I'm not going to go through your clothes."

"Fine."

There was a knock on the door and I suspected who it was.

Sadie opened it and a small squeal escaped her lips when she saw Ethan. "Hey."

He grabbed her and dipped her to the floor, kissing her deeply.

I assumed he didn't know I was there. "This isn't the roaring twenties."

He finished his kiss then helped her to a stand. "Sorry, that's how I greet my fiancée."

"In your time machine," I added.

Ethan grabbed her hand and led her to the living room. "What's going on?"

"Sadie asked me to help her pack," I answered.

Ethan looked at her. "Do you hate your brother?"

"Of course not," she said indignantly.

"Then why would you submit him to this torture?" Ethan asked.

"What happened to the sweet man that just swept me off my feet?" she asked.

Ethan smiled. "He's on break." He looked at me. "Thanks for helping her but I can take care of it. Don't worry about it."

"Phew, that's a relief," I said.

Ethan laughed. "You're welcome." He looked at me. "So how have you been?"

"Fine," I lied.

Sadie looked at me with a pitiful expression. I stared her down, making sure she didn't say anything.

Ethan didn't catch the look. "Sadie told me you've been depressed about Elisa. I'm sorry that it didn't work out."

"It's okay. Don't worry about it."

Sadie turned to him and opened her humongous mouth. "Ethan, he's in love with her. Could you talk to her?"

I glared at her. "Don't listen to her, Ethan."

Ethan looked at me. "So you mean that? You weren't just saying that?"

I took a deep breath. "This is how my night went last night. I met this beautiful girl, we had a few drinks, she invited me to her place, and before I could walk inside, I had this huge weight of guilt. Since I couldn't do it, I just left. I didn't kiss her. I didn't even touch her. I—I'm stuck."

Ethan stared at me for a long time. "So you are totally hung up on her?"

"I wish I wasn't," I said quietly.

"Let me talk to her," Ethan offered.

"Absolutely not," I snapped. "Just leave her alone. She clearly isn't ready and you can't force her to do anything. Just let it be."

Ethan sighed. "I'm afraid if I never push her, she'll be alone forever."

"And that's her decision to make," I said.

Sadie looked at me. "You've never felt this way toward anyone before. Don't just give up, Jared."

"No," I said. "She's a widow. Everything is complicated. I don't want to bother her, scare her, or manipulate her. Please leave her alone."

Ethan sighed. "I'm going to say something."

"What did I just say?" I snapped.

"I won't pressure her or make her feel uncomfortable. I know how to talk to my own sister, okay?"

I didn't say anything.

"Come with me," Ethan said.

"What?"

"I'll talk to her, and if she is ready to talk to you, I want you to be waiting."

"Outside?" I asked.

"Yeah," he answered. "If you really love her as much as you say you do, then I think we should try. I know Elisa has feelings for you. She's just scared. Maybe a little nudge is all she needs."

"I don't want to push her," I said.

"I won't," Ethan said firmly. "Don't worry about it."

"Okay."

"Are you ready?"

"We're doing this now?"

"Love can't wait," Ethan said as he stood. "Let's go."

# 3

As I stood outside in the darkness, I felt my heart accelerate. Sadie was standing next to me but neither one of us spoke. I wasn't in the mood for small talk. The cold fall air brushed through my hair and made me shiver. I didn't mind the cold. I didn't really notice.

Ethan was talking to Elisa inside. I wondered how the conversation was going. The last thing I wanted to do was scare her or make her think I was obsessed with her. I was obsessed with her but I didn't want her to know that. Minutes passed until an hour went by. If it took Ethan that long to convince Elisa to give me a chance, then she was probably going to say no. As much as it irritated me, I understood her reasoning. It was a complicated situation.

When the front door opened, I felt my heart lurch out of my chest. Ethan stepped under the porch light and I felt the depression descend. She obviously had said no. When Elisa appeared behind him, I froze. I just stared like an owl sitting in a tree. Sadie nudged my arm and snapped me out of my reverie. I approached the beginning of the stairs with my hands in the pockets of my coat. I didn't get any closer.

Elisa stared at me but said nothing. I held her gaze for a long moment.

"Come in," Ethan said.

I looked at him then back at Elisa. "Are you sure?"

She nodded.

I followed them up the stairs then stepped inside the parlor.

Ethan looked at me. "I think you two need some privacy. Sadie and I will take the kids. Have a good night."

I stared at Elisa's beautiful face and felt my hands sweat. This was really happening. She was giving me a chance. Neither one of us said anything as Ethan and Sadie grabbed the kids and their belongings. Elisa kissed them both on the head before they left. When the door was closed, she checked to make sure it was locked twice before she turned to me.

We said nothing for a long time. It wasn't awkward—just quiet.

I cleared my throat. "I'm sorry that Ethan bothered you about this. I didn't mean to pester you. I'll leave you alone if you want me to. I promise."

She crossed her arms over her chest. "I don't want you to leave, Jared."

"Okay."

She looked at the floor but said nothing.

"I want you to know that I don't expect anything from you, Elisa. I just want to spend more time with you. We can take this as slow as you want. I'll never touch you, kiss you, or make a move toward you until you're ready. You never have to worry about that."

"Okay," she said quietly.

We said nothing for a long time.

"Well, since you don't have the kids tonight, you want to go out to lunch?"

"Actually, I already ate."

I smiled. "Then let's get coffee."

She nodded. "Okay. Just let me grab my coat." She walked down the hallway and returned with a red peacoat. The color looked nice on her.

"You look great."

"Thanks."

I opened the door then ushered her out before I closed it behind us. She locked it then checked the handle twice before she finally walked away. We walked down the street a few blocks. Elisa was constantly aware of her surroundings, always looking at every person who walked by and everyone in our vicinity. She tried to be discreet about it but I noticed it. When we reached the small coffee shop, we walked inside.

We walked to a booth in the corner. It was quiet and secluded, allowing just the right amount of privacy. Music was playing in the background but it was so quiet that I could barely hear it.

When she sat down, I looked at her.

"What can I get you?"

"Just an Earl Grey tea, please."

"Sure thing."

I walked to the counter and ordered our drinks then returned to the table.

She dabbed the teabag in the hot water before she pulled it out. She liked her tea weak.

"How was your day?" I asked. I was really nervous. I couldn't think of anything better to say.

"It was good. Tommy got into my underwear drawer and threw all my delicates around the house. Ethan was beet red when he saw them on the couch."

I laughed. "That's a little awkward."

"Yeah," she said with a chuckle. "How was your day?"

"It was okay. It's a lot better now." Her brown hair curved around her face and highlighted her cheekbones. She had the most beautiful smile. Her lips were always turned up slightly so it looked like she was always smiling or smirking. She was beautiful. When I found myself staring, I looked down at my coffee.

She smiled. "Are you helping Sadie pack?"

"I'm trying to avoid it as much as possible."

"Yeah. You don't want to get into her delicates drawer."

I laughed. "Definitely not."

"Are you happy for them?"

"Uh, I wasn't at first but now I am."

She nodded. "I was skeptical in the beginning too but when I saw Ethan with her, my doubts disappeared. He's never been in a relationship before so I'm surprised he rushed into an engagement so quickly."

"Yeah. I just don't want her to get hurt."

"Ethan won't hurt her."

"I know."

"How do your parents feel about it?"

"My dad is ecstatic," I said with a laugh. "He loves Ethan—always has."

She smiled. "That's cute. What about your mom?"

"She doesn't know."

She raised an eyebrow. "She doesn't know that her daughter is engaged?"

"We aren't close to her. In fact, we don't really like her."

"Oh?"

"She abandoned all of us to pursue a job in England. She broke my dad's heart."

She nodded. "That must be hard."

"Yeah. Sadie and I became closer because of it."

"Tragedies usually bring you closer together." She looked at her tea and avoided my gaze. I knew she was thinking about her husband. "Jared, I want to ask you something."

"You can ask me anything, Elisa."

She looked at me. "Why are you so interested in me? I'm a widow with two young children. I don't have a job, a college education, or any skills. I'm just a woman with a lot of baggage."

I stared at my hands, twisting then in my grasp before I looked up. "I've never thought about it that way."

She said nothing.

"I just don't see that." I stared into her eyes. "I see a beautiful woman who's an exceptional mother. She lives for her kids and would do anything for them. She's smart, kind, and strong. And she has a smile that makes me weak."

Her eyes softened.

"I think you're amazing, Elisa. I thought it the first time I saw you."

"But do you really want to be saddled with an instant family? I'm not assuming we are going to get married or anything, but it is a possibility. There's no way that any single guy would want that."

"To be honest, I've never thought about having kids before. But I love your kids. I think they are a little crazy sometimes but they are sweet and adorable. I would be honored if you chose me as a partner to raise your children."

She said nothing.

"But I would like to have kids of my own eventually, if you were willing, of course."

She rubbed her fingers on the rim of her cup. I could tell that this conversation was making her uncomfortable. We were already talking about having kids.

"There is no specific reason why I want to be with you, Elisa. I just do. It's unexplainable and unreasonable, and it isn't dependent on any quality or trait. It just is. Therefore, it's unconditional because none of the variables can change. I just know that I want you."

She nodded. "That's very sweet."

"It's how I feel."

She sighed. "I'm never going to stop loving my husband. He'll always own a piece of my heart. I know I can make room for you but he'll always be there too. Don't you want to find someone where you would be first in their heart?"

"It doesn't bother me that you still love your husband. I know I can never replace him but I know I can make you and the kids happy. I'm willing to be patient and understanding to all of it. I wouldn't have pursued you without considering all of that."

"But wouldn't it be easier to find someone that wasn't so much work? You could have whoever you wanted—any girl off the street. Any alternative would be better."

I gave her a hard stare. "Are you done trying to get rid of me?"

She looked away.

"I've made up my mind. I want you, Elisa. There's no doubt of what I want. Now the real question is, do you want me? Are you trying to find an excuse to keep me away? We don't have to do this. There is no pressure. If you want me to leave you alone I will."

"I'm sorry, Jared. I didn't mean to sound that way. I don't want you to leave."

"I want to tell you something about myself. I've been around a lot. I've been with all kinds of girls. I've been in a few relationships, and I've had countless one night stands." She looked at me. "I'm tired of all that. I want someone that makes me feel something—makes my heart beat. That's you, Elisa. It's been you since the moment I saw you. I'm in this for the long haul. We can take this as slow as you want. I'm a patient man. I will wait."

"I—I don't know what to say."

"Don't say anything. Just stop trying to scare me off."

She smiled. "I'm sorry about that."

"It's okay."

She took a deep breath.

"And I meant what I said. I will never pressure you to do anything that you don't want to do. I want to make you as comfortable as possible."

"I know, Jared. You're a good guy."

"Ethan wouldn't let me date you if he thought otherwise."

"That's true." She drank from her tea then returned it to the table. "So what happens now?"

"We start dating?"

"Okay."

"Don't get too excited," I said with a smile.

"I'm sorry. I'm just not used to this."

"It's okay. It will get easier."

"Okay."

"Can I take you home now?"

"Sure."

We rose from the table then left the coffee shop. When we walked down the street, I placed my hands in my pockets, making it clear that I wouldn't touch her. When we reached her apartment, I walked her to the door and watched her stick her key in the lock.

"Have a good night," I said. "I'll call you tomorrow."

"You're leaving?" she asked sadly.

"Unless you want me to stay. I just didn't want to make any assumptions."

"Actually, I would prefer it if you stayed—at least until my brother comes home."

I smiled. "Of course."

She walked inside and I followed her. She locked the door and checked it twice like she always did then moved into the living room. It was obvious that she was always scared. I wanted to console her but didn't know if it was my place to say something. Perhaps it was too soon.

When she sat down on the couch, I moved to the adjacent one so I could keep my distance. I knew the best approach with her was being as unthreatening as possible.

"Anything good on television?" I asked.

She grabbed the remote and turned it on. She left it on a comedy show. I didn't stare at her so I wouldn't make her self-conscious.

"Where's your apartment?" she asked.

"Uptown," I said. "Not too far from here. You and the kids should come over sometime."

"Yeah," she said with a nod. "What do you do when you aren't working?"

"Not a lot. I'm either at the gym, hanging with my friends, or being pestered by my sister."

She smiled. "I pester Ethan. I feel bad because he has his own life, but I can't help it. I'm really glad that Sadie is so understanding of the whole situation. I know most women wouldn't agree to live with his sister and her kids, even if it is just temporary."

"Well, Sadie really loves him and I know she loves you too."

"She does?"

"And the kiddos."

"I'm going to have an amazing sister-in-law."

"And my brother-in-law is pretty cool."

"I think so."

I looked at her. "Not to make things awkward but I'm not going to be seeing anyone else during this— relationship—just in case you were worried."

"I know, Jared."

"Okay," I said as I leaned back.

We watched television for a while and just enjoyed each other's presence. I felt like we were hanging out as friends—not on a date—but I didn't mind. I knew this was how it would be for a while. Whenever I stared at her lips, I thought of other things that weren't appropriate and I shook them away. I looked at her hand on the remote and saw that she still wore her wedding ring. It didn't bother me but I knew it would if we got serious. I hoped she would remove it eventually.

The door unlocked and Ethan and Sadie stepped into the room. Both of the kids were asleep in their arms. Without making a sound, they moved down the hallway and put the children in their beds. When Ethan came back into the room, he looked at Elisa. She smiled back at him.

"Have a good night?" he asked.

Elisa nodded. "We went out for coffee."

"Cool," he said with a nod. Sadie emerged behind him and wrapped her arm around his. Her engagement ring sparkled in the light.

I rose to a stand. "Well, I should get going. Thanks for taking the kids out."

"No problem," Ethan said.

Elisa rose to her feet and walked with me toward the door.

Ethan and Sadie moved to the couch and cuddled together while they watched television.

I looked at Elisa. "Thank you for spending the evening with me."

She smiled. "Thanks for not letting me scare you off."

I laughed. "You're going to have to try a little harder than that."

"I think I'll throw in the towel."

"Good." I put my hands in my pockets and looked away.

She stepped closer to me. I wasn't sure what she was going to do. She stared into my face. She looked beautiful like she always did. The slight curve of her lips always made me think of other things. "Thanks for being so patient with me."

"I'll wait forever for you."

She wrapped her arms around my neck then hugged me. I wasn't expecting the touch at all. I flinched. I pulled my hands out of my pockets then wrapped them around her waist. I pulled her against my chest and took advantage of the opportunity to smell her hair. It smelled like coconut. Her waist felt so small in my arms. I enjoyed holding her. It was more intimate and meaningful than all my sexual transgressions. It actually meant something to me. I didn't want her to leave my arms. I liked having her there. Feeling her breasts against my chest made me think of her in sexual ways but I stopped those thoughts. If we ever slept together, it wouldn't be for a very long time. I shouldn't start thinking about it too soon.

"Good night," she whispered.

"Good night, Elisa." I pulled away then opened the front door. "I'll talk to you tomorrow."

"Okay. I look forward to it."

I smiled at her before I walked out.

# 4

When I got off work, I had twenty text messages from Sadie. I didn't have to read them to know what they said. I ignored them. I would just go by the apartment on my way home.

When I knocked on her door, she opened it immediately. "Why haven't you responded to any of my messages?" she yelled.

"Because I was at work!"

She rolled her eyes. "You have a lunch break."

"And I can only read so fast. You sent me at least twenty messages."

She pulled me inside then shut the door behind me. "So what happened?"

"Nothing."

She raised an eyebrow. "Nothing?"

"She and I talked. We are going to start dating but we're taking is slow."

She clapped her hands together. "I'm glad you figured it out."

I raised my hands. "We have a long way to go. She's still scared. I had to spend an hour trying to convince her that it was a good idea."

"Well, she hugged you. That has to mean something. She held you for a really long time. The touch definitely wasn't friendly."

I smiled. "Yeah, I think it did."

"When are you going to see her again?"

I shrugged. "Whenever she wants to see me. I don't want to suffocate her by showing her how obsessed I am."

"Don't play it too cool either. Women don't like that."

"I'll contact her every day but I'll let her initiate stuff. If I try too much too fast, it will freak her out. And the holidays are coming. That's always a hard time of year."

"I guess that makes sense."

"I understand what she needs. Let me handle it."

"So you're sure about this?"

"I've never been more sure in my life."

"How awesome would it be if you guys got married? We could all be related."

"It's actually kinda weird."

"No, it's not."

"No, it is."

"Have you told Alex?"

"No, I haven't had a chance. Are you ever going to talk to him?"

She looked uncomfortable. "If I go near him, Ethan will kill him. If he goes near me, then Ethan will kill him."

"So in either case he dies?" I couldn't hold back the smirk on my face.

"Yeah."

I sighed. "Give him a break. He was being an idiot, but I put him up to it. Don't punish him for it."

She crossed her arms over her chest. "It's not me. It's Ethan."

I rolled my eyes. "He's way too controlling."

"I would be livid if the same situation was reversed."

"But would you flip out like him?"

"Not to the same extent, but pretty close."

I turned toward the door. "I'll see you later."

"Are you going to call her?"

"Stop gossiping like we're girlfriends."

"I'm not gossiping!"

I laughed. "I'll see you later."

After I left her apartment, I went to mine a few floors up. After I changed, I hit the gym and did an intense session of weights. I went to the gym often but I wasn't always religious about it. I was already fit and tone, but I wanted to become more bulky now that I was with Elisa.

When I came home, I showered and threw my dirty clothes in the hamper. I stared at my phone for a while before I picked it up and called her.

"Hey," she said.

"Hey," I said with a smile. "What are you doing? Picking up delicates from around the apartment?"

She laughed. "No. We just went to the park so I had to give the kids a bath. They were filthy."

"Was Ethan with you?"

"Yes."

I nodded even though she couldn't see me.

"You want to come over tonight? Have dinner with us?"

I smiled. I was excited that she invited me over. "That sounds great. Do you need me to pick anything up on the way?"

"No. I have everything."

"I'll see you soon."

"Okay. Bye."

"Bye."

I pulled on a sweater and a pair of jeans then headed to her townhouse. When I arrived, I could smell the chicken on the stove and the sauce in the pan. I wasn't used to home cooking until Sadie moved in down stairs from my apartment. I usually just ate out. I was too lazy to learn how to cook.

Ethan clapped me on the shoulder. "Nice to have you over."

"Thanks," I said. "Is Sadie coming?"

"No. She's packing her drawers and stuff."

"Oh, okay."

Elisa emerged from the kitchen wearing a dirty apron. There was a small amount of sauce on her cheek. When I reached up to wipe it away, I steadied my hand, knowing I shouldn't touch her.

"Hey," she said with smile. She stared at my hand. "Do I have something on my face?"

"Yeah," I said with a laugh.

"Could you get it for me?"

I wiped it with my thumb then placed it into my mouth. "Yum. That tastes good."

She blushed. "Thanks for coming."

"Do you need any help?"

"No. I got it."

"Okay."

Tommy walked over to me and pulled on my pant leg. "Hi."

"Hey," I said as I picked him up. "What's going on, Tommy?"

He pointed at his toys. "My cars."

I looked at them. "They're nice."

"I asked Mommy for more for Christmas."

"Well, hopefully you were a good boy this year."

"Mommy says I'm always good."

I smiled at him. "I'm sure that's true."

"What about me?" a small voice said.

I looked down and saw Becky. "Hey, honey."

She reached her hands up to me, wanting me to pick her up. I grabbed her from the floor and held them both. My arms were sore from the gym but I ignored the discomfort. The more I was around these kids, the more I adored them. I carried them into the living room then sat on the couch with them. Ethan handed me a beer then sat next to me.

Elisa emerged from the kitchen then stopped when she saw me. I wasn't sure how she would react. Last time she saw me bonding with her kids, she looked like she was going to cry with guilt. She smiled at me for a moment then returned to the kitchen. That went better than I expected.

After she set the table, she turned to us. "Dinner is ready."

I rose from the couch then carried the kids to the table. I placed them in their booster seats and placed the napkins in their laps. Then I sat between them so I could reach them easily.

Elisa placed the food on the table then sat across from me. She smiled at me for a moment before she started to dish out the chicken and rice. Ethan sat beside her and started to inhale his food.

As soon as I tasted the food, my mouth began to water. "This is amazing, Elisa."

"Thanks," she said with a smile.

I turned to Ethan. "I'm jealous you get this treatment every day."

"It's a good exchange for all my help," he said as he ate.

Elisa ate half of her food but couldn't finish it all. I noticed that she was very thin. I liked her body and thought she was perfect, but she was also on the thinner side. I would have to change that.

The kids ate quietly. Becky spilled rice everywhere. It stuck to her fingers and her lips. I used my napkin to wipe it away and cleaned up the mess. When we were done, Elisa grabbed the plates and brought them to the sink. I cleaned up the kids then returned them to the living room where they played on the floor with their toys. Then I went to the kitchen and helped with the dishes.

"Jared, you don't need to do that."

"You cooked so I'll clean."

"That's sweet but unnecessary."

"At least let me help."

"Okay."

I helped her scrub the dishes then placed them in the dishwater. Then I helped her wrap the food and put in the refrigerator. When the cleaning was done, we returned to the living room. As soon as I sat down, Tommy crawled into my lap and started playing with his cars. Elisa sat on the other couch and watched us for a long time. Ethan and I stared at the television until Tommy fell asleep on my lap. Becky climbed on the couch and fell asleep shortly afterwards.

Ethan yawned. "I'm going to bed."

"Goodnight," I said.

"Night," he said. He looked at his sister. "You want me to put them to bed?"

"Don't worry about it," she said.

"Okay." He walked down the hall.

I rose from the couch and carried Tommy in my arms. "I'll put him in bed."

She grabbed Becky and followed me. After I put Tommy in bed, I watched her put Becky to sleep before she left and closed the door behind her. When we walked back into the living room, I grabbed my jacket to leave.

"You're great with them," she said.

"Thanks." I was glad she noticed.

She crossed her arms over her chest. "You don't have to leave."

I stared at her. "It's getting late. I don't want to wear out my welcome."

She stepped closer to me then wrapped her arms around my neck. When she pressed her forehead against mine, I felt my heart beat like a drum. She stared at my lips and I stared at hers. I felt the tension in the air increase as I held her in my arms. I wanted to kiss her but I knew I shouldn't. It seemed like she wanted me to but I was afraid I was going to rush it and confuse her. When she leaned toward me, I moved my lips to her forehead and kissed her gently.

She stilled as she felt my lips on her skin.

"Thanks for having me."

"Yeah," she whispered.

"I'll talk to you tomorrow."

"Okay."

I kissed her on the forehead again. "Good night."

"Good night."

I opened the door then walked out. I heard it close and lock behind me.

# 5

"Let's go out tonight," Alex said on the phone.

"And do what?"

"Get laid. You never told me how that chick was."

"Because I didn't sleep with her."

"You struck out?"

"No," I said. "I ditched her."

"What? Why? She was fine."

"I want someone else."

He laughed. "Wow. You ditched one girl for another one the same night—smooth."

"No. Elisa and I are—talking."

"That girl you're hung up on?"

"Yeah," I said with a smile.

"Since when?"

"The other day."

"So you aren't single anymore?"

"Yes—no—it's complicated."

"What? So can you pick up chicks with me tonight or not?"

"No," I said quickly.

"So she finally came around?"

"We are taking it slow."

"Doesn't she have kids?"

"Yeah. They're great."

"Wow."

"What?"

"You just don't seem like the kind of guy to want someone else's kids."

"Well, I am, apparently."

"Have you talked to Sadie about me?" Alex asked.

"I mentioned it."

"And?"

"Yeah—she doesn't want to talk to you."

"Her or that piece of shit boyfriend she has?"

I sighed. "I understand why you don't like the guy but don't say things like that about him. He's going to be my brother-in-law soon."

"Not you too," he said with sigh.

"He's a good guy and he makes my sister happy. Let it go."

"I just want to be her friend again. I want her back."

"It doesn't sound like it's going to happen."

"Maybe I should talk to Ethan."

"No," I said quickly. "Definitely not."

"What if you and I both talked to him?"

"You think I can protect you?" I asked incredulously.

"He won't throw a punch if you ask him not to. You guys are practically family, right?"

"I guess."

"Just do this for me. I really don't want to get cut out because I can't see Sadie anymore. Please."

"Okay. I'll ask."

"When?"

"I'm meeting them now."

"Let me know how it goes."

"Okay. See ya."

"Bye."

I walked down the street until I reached the diner. I was meeting Sadie, Ethan, and my dad for an early dinner. I wanted to invite Elisa and the kids but I thought that was too soon. I'm sure it would've freaked her out and made her run away.

When I walked inside, they were already sitting down.

"Hey, Dad," I said as I hugged him.

"Hey," he said with a smile. "How was work?"

"Good now that it's over."

Ethan nodded. "It was a long day."

I sat down next to my dad, across from Sadie and Ethan.

"Hey," I said to my sister.

She smiled at me.

My dad looked at the menu. "So I heard you're seeing some girl—and she's a lot better than Suzie."

I glared at Sadie then looked at my dad. I didn't want to discuss Elisa that soon. She had two kids from her previous marriage. I wasn't sure if my dad would be supportive. "Yes, she's Ethan's sister."

"Then she must be great."

I nodded. "I like her."

"When am I going to meet her?"

"Eventually, I hope."

"Tell her not to be scared of me. I'm sure I'll love her."

I nodded. I wasn't so sure of that. "Well, there's something you should know about her."

He raised an eyebrow.

"She has two kids."

"She's divorced?"

"No, she's a widow."

"Oh? That's horrible. I'm so sorry."

"Yeah," I said. "It's pretty sad."

He looked at me. "Well, this sounds complicated. Are you sure you want to get involved in that?"

"Yes," I said. "I've thought about it for a long time."

He stared at me, gauging my sincerity. "If you're sure."

"I am."

"Well, then I look forward to meeting her—and her kids. They might be my grandkids someday."

I smiled at him, grateful for his support. "Thanks, Dad."

He looked at Sadie. "So when's the wedding?" he asked happily.

She shrugged. "We haven't decided yet."

"What did the girls think?"

Sadie was quiet for a moment. "They were shocked."

"That isn't surprising," my dad said.

"But they were supportive eventually," Sadie continued. "After Natascia rambled on for hours, I asked her to be my maid of honor and she finally calmed down."

Ethan smiled. "I'm glad they are on board."

"Have you told your mom?" my dad asked.

"Uh, no," Sadie answered.

"Why not?" he asked.

"Well, I haven't had a chance to call her," she explained.

He shook his head. "She doesn't even know about Ethan, does she?"

She stuttered again. "Uh, no."

I saw Ethan stare at her, clearly disappointed that their relationship was still a secret in some way.

Sadie caught the look. "I'll tell her soon."

"Is she invited?" I asked.

"Uh, I wasn't planning on it," Sadie said.

My dad looked at her. "Sadie, you have to invite your mother."

"Why?" she snapped. "It's my day and I don't want her there."

"Sadie, that would kill her."

She shook her head. "She doesn't care about anyone but herself. I want people I actually care about to be there—people who care about me."

"Don't be cold," my father said.

"Why aren't you being cold?" she snapped. "She took off and abandoned all of us. I don't care if it hurts her feelings. She's lucky that I return her phone calls and humor her at all."

He stared at her for a moment. "If it doesn't bother me, it shouldn't bother you."

She stood up from her seat. "I'm done talking about this." She walked away and entered the bathroom.

I sighed. I figured Sadie would act that way. Ever since she found out that Mom totally abandoned Dad and ended their marriage without any remorse, she pretty much hated Mom. I was surprised she even considered taking that job at all. I wasn't shocked that she didn't want Mom to be there. To be honest, I didn't want her to be there either.

Ethan ran his fingers through his hair. "I'll talk to her."

My dad nodded. "Thank you."

"Yeah," Ethan said. "She's just emotional right now. I'll bring it up tomorrow."

My dad moved from his seat. "I'm going to visit the bathroom as well." He turned and left.

I looked at Ethan. I guess it was a good time to bring it up. "So, there's something I wanted to discuss."

"Oh—oh. The older brother talk?"

I laughed. "No. It's about something else."

"What's up?"

"It's about Alex."

His smile dropped and the light in his eyes disappeared. He clenched his fist on the table. "I hope you're about to tell me that he was hit by a car and passed away from a violent death."

I could tell how the conversation was going to go. "He doesn't want to lose Sadie from his life forever and—"

"Too fucking bad."

"Just hear me out."

He continued to clench his fists.

"Alex respects your engagement and your position as her boyfriend. He just wants her friendship. He regrets everything that happened. Please don't ostracize him from our lives. He's sorry."

Ethan said nothing for a moment. "No."

"Come on."

"Why should I trust that fucker? He tried to steal my girl."

"And it didn't work. He's over it. Give him another chance."

"I don't trust him."

"That's fine. Can he be around Sadie if you're there? That's reasonable."

"How can you be friends with a punk like that?"

"He's a good guy. You just didn't see him in his best light."

"I'm sure," he said sarcastically.

"Come on. It would be weird if he wasn't at the wedding. He isn't trying to get with Sadie anymore."

He sighed. "I'll consider it."

I stared at him. "For how long?"

"Fine. He can see her as long as I'm present. If I'm not there, he better stay the fuck away from her."

I nodded. "That's fair."

"And generous."

"Thank you."

"Did he put you up to this?"

"It was a joint effort."

"Why would you want him around your sister anyway? He obviously has no respect for her or who she cares about."

I sighed. "I understand why you feel that way but he really is a good guy. You just came in at his darkest moment. He's been in love with Sadie since I can remember. When you came into the picture, he panicked."

"He had all the time in the world to make a move. Why did he choose now?"

I shrugged. "He was just too nervous about how she would react. When he realized he was missing his chance, he finally went for it."

"That still isn't my problem."

"I know. I'm just explaining everything."

Ethan looked away. "I still don't trust him. If I find out that he pursued her when she was alone, I swear to god I'll kill him."

I could tell by the anger in his eyes that he was being serious. I felt bad for Alex. He got himself into a bad situation. "It's my fault too. I'm the one that set up that dinner."

"I'm still not happy about that."

"Well, you can't hold him accountable for that one. I was in the wrong."

"You better not pull anything like that again."

"Are you threatening me now?"

He sighed. "We are family now, and I never want to hurt you or disrespect you, but Sadie means more to me than I can possibly express. If anything jeopardized her from being in my arms, I wouldn't care less who you are. I will fight to keep her."

"Well, I'm not your enemy so you never have to worry about that."

"Good."

Sadie and my dad returned from the bathroom at the same time. Sadie still looked mad and my father looked uncomfortable.

Ethan kissed her on the cheek. "Ready to go, baby?"

She nodded.

Ethan left the cash on the table. I picked up half of it then handed it back to him. I added my half to the pile. I knew he didn't mind paying for things but he had a family to take care of. I would pay for all of it but I didn't want to emasculate him in front of my father.

We said our goodbyes then left the restaurant. I headed back to my apartment then collapsed on the couch. I went to the gym before dinner and I pushed it so hard that I threw up in the locker room. I wanted to be as muscular as possible. I was already strong and fit, but I wanted Elisa to feel safe with me.

My phone rang and I grabbed it from my pocket. It was Elisa. "Hey," I said with a smile. I wasn't going to call her because I didn't want to suffocate her. I was glad that she reached out to me.

"Hey. How are you?"

"Good. You?"

"Good. How was dinner? Ethan just told me you went."

"It was okay. Sadie and my dad got into an argument about inviting my mom to the wedding. It was a little bit tense after that."

"I'm sorry to hear that."

"Yeah. My dad is too nice. I don't want our mom there either. She didn't want to be part of our lives for seven years. Sadie's wedding day shouldn't make a difference."

"I agree."

I laughed. "Sorry, I didn't mean to dump all my personal bullshit on you."

"It's okay."

"How are the little ones?"

"Tommy has been quiet today. I think he's getting sick. Becky got a gold star in her art class so she's been drawing pictures and taping them all over the walls."

I chuckled. "That's cute."

"Yeah, it is."

I fell silent, unsure what to say. I wanted to see her but I'd spent the previous two nights with her. She might not have wanted to see me.

"So, Ethan and Sadie offered to watch the kids tonight."

That caught my attention. "Yeah?"

"Yeah. Maybe we can do something."

"I would love to see you, Elisa. Can I take you out to dinner then for drinks?"

She was quiet for a moment. "How about we stay at your place?"

I felt my heart accelerate. "My place?"

"Yeah. I've never seen your apartment."

I swallowed the lump in my throat. Maybe I was jumping to conclusions, but when a chick wanted to see my apartment that usually meant she wanted me to fuck her. I shook my head. I couldn't think like that. Elisa wasn't like that. She seemed genuinely interested in just seeing where I lived. "Yeah. I'll come get you when you're ready."

"I'm ready now."

"Great. I'll be there soon."

"Okay."

"Bye."

"Bye."

I hung up the phone then left the apartment. We were so close to kissing the other night and I wondered if she wanted that to happen today. I really, really wanted to kiss her. Her lips always looked wet and delicious. I had never been more attracted to a woman than I was to her. When I thought about seeing her naked, I had to force the thoughts back. The arousal would consume me. I was always hard when I was around her even if we were just sitting on opposite couches. I felt like an adolescent pervert.

When I reached the apartment, Elisa answered it with a smile on her face. She wore tight jeans and a black blouse. Her shiny hair fell across her shoulders. She looked amazing.

"You're as beautiful as ever," I blurted.

She smiled. "Thank you." She closed the door behind her and locked it.

"Does Ethan know where you're going?"

"Yes."

I raised an eyebrow. "And he's okay with that?"

"Don't worry about him, Jared. He finally stopped being psycho," she said with a laugh.

"Phew."

She laughed again. "Sadie is almost settled in the apartment."

"I'm glad I didn't have to help her."

We walked down the street in the darkness. When Elisa wrapped her arm through mine, I almost stopped. Her affection was always welcome but it still surprised me. When she hugged me, I almost fainted. I liked feeling her small arm next to mine. She clung to me like I was her boyfriend. I really liked the idea of that. I pulled my hand out of my pocket and wrapped it around her waist, holding her close to me. When she smiled at me, warmth radiated through my body.

"Are you okay with Sadie moving in?" I asked.

"Yes, of course. She's always welcome with us."

"Really?"

"I just feel bad that she has to stay with us. Ethan has his own life. I want him to move out and be happy with her. Just because Tom died doesn't mean he has to sacrifice everything for me. I do appreciate everything he's done, but I want him to be happy.

"Does he know that?"

"I told him many times. I don't want him to lose Sadie over it. He said she doesn't mind waiting a year. They just couldn't stand to be apart during that time. As soon as the kids start school, I'm getting a job and kicking them out. My brother pushed me to date you, knowing how hard it was for me. Now I need to push him, help him get over the guilt he has.

"A year isn't that long."

"No, it's not.

"You aren't afraid to be on your own?"

"No. I can handle it. I've had enough time to move past Tom's death. I think I can handle a full time job and my two babies. Life goes on. And even if I couldn't, I would never tell Ethan that. I need him to leave and make a life with Sadie. The children and I will figure it out.

"No matter what happens between us, I'll always be here for you. If you ever need anything, let me know."

"My children are lucky they have so many people to love them."

"Well, it's hard not to. They're pretty adorable."

She blushed. "Thanks."

We arrived at my building then took the elevator to my floor. I caressed her knuckles with my thumb while I held her hand. Her skin was soft and smooth. I wondered what the rest of her body felt like. I stopped those thoughts before they led elsewhere.

When we walked inside the apartment, I immediately felt the tension in the air. We had been alone together before but never in a setting like this. No one would walk in on us or hear us. A small child wouldn't run down the hallway and see us.

Elisa looked around the room. "It's nice."

"Uh, thanks." My apartment was ordinary. Sadie added some decorations so it wouldn't look so much like a man cave but it still didn't feel like a home.

She removed her coat then hung it over the couch. Her blouse fit her tightly and highlighted the curve of her breasts. I looked away so I wouldn't start drooling like an idiot.

"What do you want to do?" she asked.

"Uh," I stuttered. There were a lot of things I wanted to do. "Wanna watch a movie?"

"Sure."

I opened the refrigerator and grabbed a bottle of wine. I poured the glasses then carried them to the couch. She sat next to me, right next to me. I could feel her thigh against mine. She was a lot more intimate than she ever was before. I liked it but I was frightened at the same time.

When I glanced down to her finger, I saw that she still wore her wedding ring. I didn't like the sight.

We leaned back in our seats and started to watch the movie. She leaned close to me and placed her hand on my thigh. There was a bulge in my pants and I hoped she didn't notice it. I felt like a horny teenager that was too nervous to move. If she was any other girl, I would have slept with her already. But she wasn't any other girl. She was the love of my life.

Elisa moved even closer to me. I could feel her breaths fall on my neck. I wanted to kiss her, rub her tongue against mine, but I held back. I told her that I wouldn't physically pursue her and I intended to keep my word. She would have to initiate it if she wanted it to happen. I refused to pressure her.

"Jared?"

"Yeah?" I said as I looked at her. Her eyes reflected the light from the television. They were blue and beautiful, and reminded me of the ocean. They were bright from their own innate light. I was hypnotized by her features. She was so beautiful, perfect. I wish I had met her a long time ago. I wished that I were her husband and the father of her kids. I swallowed the lump in my throat as I waited for her to speak. I didn't know what she was going to say.

"Kiss me."

I cupped her face and pressed my forehead against hers. I stared at her lips for a long time before I leaned in and pressed my mouth against hers. Her lips were soft and wet. When I caressed them, I felt the fire ignite within me. I never felt that way when I kissed someone. My heart physically hurt from the pleasure I was feeling. I could feel all my love for her explode.

I was gentle with every kiss, wanting to feel every curve of her lips with my own. She was an amazing kisser. When she inserted her tongue within me, I actually shivered. She tasted sweet like assorted fruit on a summer day. I ran my fingers through her hair and felt the softness with my fingertips. It felt like silk.

Elisa placed her hand on my shoulder then dragged it down my chest, feeling the muscles underneath my shirt. I flexed so she could feel my strength and size. I wanted her to know that I was strong, that I could protect her. Her hands touched my hard stomach then glided back to my hair. I hoped she liked what she felt. All the other girls seemed to enjoy it.

The sound of our wet kisses landed on my ears. The quiet smacking and flickering of our tongues was arousing. A small moan would escape her lips every few seconds. I loved hearing the sound. I wanted to listen to it on a grander scale while I made love to her. I pushed the thought back. I couldn't think like that—especially now.

She gently pulled me forward as she lay down. I climbed on top of her then leaned over her, kissing her the entire way. I felt her breasts press against my chest. They were soft and firm. She wrapped one of her legs around mine, holding me to her.

I cupped her face while I kissed her, feeling the softness of her cheeks with my fingers. She was so gorgeous and I couldn't believe she was kissing me. I loved her so much. I didn't understand why, but I understood that I did. She was a strong woman who had suffered so much, but she still smiled every day like she was happy. She was sweet and caring, a wonderful mother. I fell for her the moment I saw her. My love wasn't just a physical desire for her. I loved being around her and just talking to her.

Her hands glided up my shirt and felt the skin underneath. She felt my powerful chest and moaned as her fingertips trailed over the muscles. I flexed again so she could feel every curve. She moaned again and I felt triumphant.

She grabbed the rim of my shirt then pulled it over my head. This was something I didn't expect to happen. Stunned, I let her pull the material away. She broke our kiss and stared at my body for a moment. She must have liked what she saw because she started kissing me again, feeling my strong back with her fingers. I thought about removing her shirt but I refused to do it. I didn't mind taking off my clothes but I wouldn't be able to control myself if she removed hers. I wouldn't be a gentleman anymore.

She grabbed the rim of my pants and unbuttoned them. I had no idea what was going on. When she started to pull them down, I steadied her hand. "Elisa."

"What?" she asked as she kissed me.

"We can't do this." I couldn't believe what I was saying. I really wanted this to happen. I was stronger than I thought.

"And why not?"

"Because I'm in love with you."

She pulled away and stared at me. Her eyes were soft.

I met her look. "If we do this then everything will change. I won't be the same man. I'll be jealous, controlling, obsessive, and protective. I'll need to be with you all the time. You won't be able to get rid of me because I'll never leave. If you make love to me, I will possess you completely. You will be mine and no one else's. This is very serious. I would be giving myself completely to you, becoming vulnerable to you. I'm already lovestruck over you, but it would be a million times more intense. If you make love to me, you are committing to me, telling me that you love me. There's nothing I want more but only if you're ready." I rubbed my nose against hers. "So, are you ready? This has happened really fast. If you need more time to get to know me before you let me possess you completely, I understand. It's frightening. I've never felt this way for someone before."

She ran her fingers through my hair while she looked at me. "I—I don't know."

I felt my heart fall. That isn't the response I was hoping for. I kissed her forehead. "That's okay. I don't want you to rush into something you aren't ready for."

"But I feel like I'm ready."

"If you have any doubt then you aren't."

"I'm just afraid that I'm going to get scared and run away."

I nodded. "Then please don't do this with me. I couldn't recover from the pain. I'm already madly in love with you."

She rubbed my cheek with her palm.

"Before we got together, I took a girl back to her apartment to have sex with her." Her eyes widened as she listened to me. "I wanted to forget about you and move on, but I couldn't sleep with her. All I thought about was you. I just walked away."

"Jared."

"I love you, Elisa. Please don't hurt me."

"Okay," she whispered. "I won't."

I kissed her. "Thank you."

"So we shouldn't do this?"

"No."

"But I still want to—fool around. Is that okay?"

I smiled. "That sounds okay to me."

She grabbed my face and kissed me again. After a moment, her hands returned to the rim of my pants and she pulled them down. Now that I knew we wouldn't have sex, I wasn't so nervous. She ran her hands down my body then placed them on my ass, squeezing gently.

I decided to move this into the bedroom. I cradled her in my arms then carried her into my bedroom while I kissed her the entire way. When I laid her down, she pulled me on top of her. My bedroom was dark and quiet. I could hear every breath and every caress of her tongue. I loved the sound.

She grabbed the rim of my boxer shorts and pulled them down. I wasn't embarrassed to let her see me naked, but I wasn't sure why she wanted to. When I was completely naked, she broke our kiss and stared at me. "Jared, you're so fucking hot." She stared at my cock while she felt the muscles of my chest and stomach. She moaned as she stared at me.

"Thank you," I said with a smile. "I'm all yours."

She kissed my neck then trailed her kisses to my chest. I watched her for a moment, loving the feel of her kisses. "Jared, I want you inside me."

I felt my skin prickle. "I know. It will happen eventually."

She grabbed my face and kissed me again. I could feel the arousal coursing through her as she kissed me. Her mouth was aggressive as it possessed me. She wanted me— bad. It turned me on so much that this beautiful woman was begging me to sleep with her. I knew she didn't mean it. She was just emotional right then. If she was naked and lying on top of me, I would probably beg her to sleep with me too.

While I kissed her, I unbuttoned her jeans then slid my hand down to her pussy. She opened her legs farther as I glided to the source of her arousal. She was so wet. Her panties were soaked with her fluid. The knowledge almost made me come. I started to rub her clit gently. She immediately started to moan while she kissed me harder. Her hands ran wild across my body.

"Jared," she whispered.

I inserted two fingers inside her while I rubbed her clit at the same time.

She was panting and shaking for me. I knew it wouldn't take long to get her off. She broke our kiss and stared at my body while I fingered her. She gripped my shoulders tightly as she started to come.

"Elisa," I whispered. "Come for me."

"Oh—god," she yelled.

I rubbed her clit harder, making her orgasm intense.

"Jared—oh."

"Yeah."

When her legs stopped shaking, I knew she was done. She leaned her head back as she ran her hands across my body. "Jared, you're amazing."

"I just like making you feel good."

"You're so fucking hot."

I smiled. "I'm glad you think so."

She grabbed my cock and started to massage it. "You're so big."

I stiffened as she rubbed my shaft. "Elisa."

"I want you to feel as good as I feel."

I pulled her hand away. "No."

She returned it to my cock. "Yes."

I bit my lip while she rubbed me.

She leaned over and opened my night stand drawer. She searched through it until she found a Vaseline bottle.

"How did you know that was in there?"

"Every single guy has one," she said with a smile.

I smiled.

She opened it and placed the fluid on her hand, I felt my heart accelerate as I watched her. I was so horny that I didn't feel ashamed. I wanted her to jerk me off. Feeling her wet pussy and watching her get off made me want to come. I wasn't being a gentleman anymore. My hormones had taken over.

She rubbed the slippery lotion all over my cock and I moaned loudly.

Elisa grabbed my face and started to kiss me while she jerked me hard. It felt so good I thought I was going to come. With every kiss of her lips, I was crumbling. She knew exactly what she was doing. She squeezed the tip then moved all the way down to the base of my balls.

I pressed my forehead against hers. "Elisa." I fisted her hair while I started to move with her hand. I felt my orgasm breach the surface. My breathing had increased and sweat dripped from my chest. "I'm—I'm gonna come."

"Come on," she whispered.

"I'm almost there."

She jerked me harder.

"Fuck—I'm coming."

She used her other hand to catch my come while she continued to rub me, jerking all the orgasm out of me. When I was completely done, I didn't move. I continued to hover over her, overcoming my sudden moment of fatigue.

She reached over and opened my drawer again, pulling out a roll of toilet paper.

I smiled. "I can tell that you grew up with guys."

She wiped her hand then cleaned me off. "I caught them a few times," she with a disgusted face.

When I was dry, I lay down beside her. She immediately cuddled next to me and I wrapped my arms around her. I felt dirty but satisfied at the same time. I could smell the coconut scent of her hair and it calmed me.

She ran her hand over my chest. "I could eat you."

I kissed her forehead. "Anytime."

"You work out a lot?"

"Every day."

"That explains a lot."

"I can't wait to see what you look like."

"I hope you like it."

"I can promise you that I will."

She kissed my neck gently then rested her head on my chest. "Can we sleep together for a while?"

"Sure," I said. I grabbed my alarm from the nightstand and set it for a few hours later. "I want to make sure we wake up. I don't want to take you home in the morning. That would be inappropriate."

"Ethan knows it will happen eventually."

"Well, eventually isn't now." I moved next to her and wrapped her in my arms.

She sighed happily as she cuddled in my arms.

"Elisa?"

"Yeah?"

"Thank you for taking a chance on me."

# 6

"So, what happened?" Alex asked as he spotted me on the bench.

"Ethan agreed."

"He did?"

"I was surprised too." I did a few reps before my arms started to shake. Alex took the bar and racked it.

"That's a lot of weight. Why are you doing so much?"

I was quiet for a moment. "No reason."

"So I can talk to Sadie again?"

"Only when he's around."

"I knew there would be a catch," he said with a sigh. "Can I talk to her today?"

"I guess. I don't know what she's doing."

"Is she living with him yet?"

"Yeah. She just got settled."

"Can you take me over there?"

"Can you go by yourself?"

"Well, what if Ethan changes his mind when he sees me."

I laughed. "You're such a pussy."

"Hey. I like my face the way it is. It's a lot harder to pick up chicks when you only have one eye and two teeth."

"Good point," I said. "So you're trying to move on?"

He shrugged. "I guess. I wish I went for Sadie when I had the chance."

"If it makes you feel better, I don't think she would have wanted you anyway."

"Yeah, I feel loads better now," he said sarcastically.

"Sorry."

"Can we go now?"

"Yeah. Let's shower and head over."

We left the gym and went into the locker room. After we were done, we walked up the block until we reached the small townhouse. I was wearing the suit I wore to work, and Alex was wearing slacks and a collared shirt. I could tell that he was nervous because of how quiet he was.

I knocked on the door and waited for someone to answer it.

When I saw Elisa open the door with a smile on her face, my heart melted. "Hi."

"Hey." Without thinking, I wrapped my arms around her and kissed her gently. She reciprocated my affection immediately.

She rubbed her nose against mine before she pulled away. "What brings you here?"

"Other than seeing my gorgeous girlfriend? Well, we wanted to talk to Ethan and Sadie. Are they here?"

"Yeah. Come in."

Alex and I walked inside.

She shook his hand while she smiled at him. "Hi, I'm Elisa."

He smiled back. "Alex. I've heard a lot about you."

"I hope they were good things that you heard," she said with a glance at me. She and I were both thinking the same thing, remembering our foreplay last night.

"Very good things," he said with a nod.

"I'll be right back," she said as she walked down the hallway.

Alex looked at me. "Getting serious?"

"I think so."

"Have you slept with her?"

I glared at him. "Even if I did, I wouldn't tell you."

He raised an eyebrow. "Don't get psycho on me. You tell me about every girl you sleep with. Sorry, I didn't know that fact didn't apply to Elisa."

"Sorry," I said.

"You better be."

Ethan walked down the hall with Sadie trailing behind him. He completely ignored me and stared at Alex with demonic fire spewing out of his eyes. I would hate to be Alex right then. I've been the recipient of that stare a few times. I was suddenly distracted when I felt Elisa wrap her arm around my waist and move close to me. I stared down at her in surprise. I loved her affection. I kissed her on the forehead then wrapped my arm around her. Sadie smiled at us before she looked at Alex.

Elisa watched Ethan glare at Alex. "Is there going to be a fight?"

"Not sure yet," her brother answered.

"Well, remember your niece and nephew," she said.

Ethan sighed. "Let's go outside."

Alex swallowed the lump in his throat before he walked through the front door. We all moved outside until we were on the top step.

Alex placed his hands in his pockets and looked Ethan in the eye. "I just want to talk to Sadie."

"Well, talk," Ethan said. He was still standing in front of Sadie, completely blocking her from view.

Sadie walked around and stood in front of him. Like a mother bear with her cub, Ethan wrapped his arm around her waist and held her to his chest. She rolled her eyes even though he couldn't see her. "This is the most privacy you're going to get," she said to Alex.

"That's okay," he said. He was quiet for a moment. I felt bad for the guy.

I felt Elisa's breast against my chest as she moved into me. I became very distracted with the touch. I had the flashback of fingering her and her jerking me and I felt the bulge in my pants. She was so gorgeous. I couldn't look directly at her because it hurt my eyes. I leaned down and rubbed my nose against hers, staring into her eyes. I could stare at them all day. I kissed her gently then leaned toward her ear. "You make me weak in the knees, Elisa."

"You make my heart weak."

"That shouldn't be a problem because I'll never break it."

She smiled at me and I felt my heart melt.

"Well, spit it out," Ethan snapped.

His words snapped me out of my lovestruck moment.

Alex ran his fingers through his hair while he looked at Sadie. "I'm sorry about everything. I really am. I was being a jerk to you and I apologize. I've had feelings for you for a long time, and when I saw you get with Ethan, it broke my heart. Love does crazy things to people." Sadie's eyes softened as she listened to him. "I really don't want to lose you from my life. I respect your relationship with Ethan and I'm happy for you. Please don't cut me out. We've been friends for so long. I promise that I won't touch you, pursue you, or make you uncomfortable in any way. Please stop hating me."

"Alex, I don't hate you."

"I do," Ethan said.

"And neither does Ethan," she said.

"She's lying," Ethan said.

She rolled her eyes. "Ignore him."

"That would be unwise."

She turned around and looked at him. "Would you shut up already? I'm yours—he gets it."

Elisa and I chuckled quietly to ourselves. I leaned toward her. "That's going to be me but a hundred times worse."

She stared at me. "I guess we shouldn't sleep together for as long as possible."

I groaned.

She smiled. "I think it's cute."

"That's a relief."

"And annoying," she added.

"Well, get used to it. It's going to happen."

She sighed. "Okay."

Ethan was quiet for a moment before he nodded.

Sadie turned around. "Like I said, I don't hate you, Alex. I was just hurt and uncomfortable by your actions."

"And I understand why. I'm very sorry. It won't happen again."

"I don't want to cut you out either."

"So you forgive me?" he asked hopefully.

"Of course," she said with a smile. She moved from Ethan's arms to hug him, but Ethan held her back.

"Are you fucking kidding me right now?" Ethan snapped.

Alex sighed. "How about a handshake?"

Ethan said nothing.

Sadie glared at Ethan before she reached out and hugged him, defying Ethan. "It's behind us."

Ethan glared at Alex. "I still don't want you alone with her. If I catch you, I'll make you regret it."

"Don't you think that's unreasonable?" Sadie asked.

"No," Ethan snapped.

Alex nodded. "As long as we're friends again, I'm fine with that."

Sadie smiled. "Okay."

Alex stepped back. "Well, I guess I'll see you later then." He looked at me and waited for me to say goodbye. When I took a step forward, Elisa tightened her grip on me and held me close.

I smiled at her. "I'll catch you later, man."

Alex nodded. "Okay. I'll see you later." He walked away and disappeared down the road.

Ethan and Sadie walked inside the house, arguing the entire way.

"Why do you have to be a crazy asshole all the time?" she yelled.

"Because you're my wife!"

"Not yet—thankfully."

"What did you say to me?"

"You can be a little too psychotic at times."

Their words feel silent. I assumed that they were kissing.

Elisa smiled at me. "That doesn't sounds so bad."

I rubbed my nose against hers. "Good."

"Let's go inside."

We walked into the house. The kids were still playing on the floor. Becky was brushing the hair of her pony, and Tommy was watching a cartoon. When I looked at the walls, I saw all the paintings.

"They are ridiculous, huh?" she asked.

"Adorable," I whispered.

"I don't have a scrapbook big enough to keep them all."

I sat down on the couch and leaned back. I wasn't expecting Elisa to sit by me but she did. I wrapped my arm around her shoulder while she leaned into me. We watched the kids for a long time while we sat together. I had visions of my life with her, a life of a stepfather. I realized it was something I really wanted. I couldn't wait for it to happen.

# 7

The next two months were amazing. Elisa and I saw each other almost every day. I took her to the movies a few times, out to dinner, coffee, and went on family trips to the park, museums, and to the toy store.

It was cold in Manhattan. The snow piled up on the sidewalk. Steam rose from the buildings into the sky. The homeless people on the streets bundled up and tried to bear the cold weather. I usually hated winter time but I loved it that year. I loved spending the holidays with Elisa.

She and I still hadn't slept together but we fooled around every chance we got. I fingered her too many times to count and she was a pro at jerking me off. As much as I loved the hand action, I really want more from her. I wanted to be inside her and finalize our relationship. I wanted to make her mine forever. But I knew I couldn't rush it. I just had to wait.

She didn't talk about her husband, which I was thankful for. Not because I didn't care about her pain and her feelings, but because I was in love with her and I didn't want to think about her loving anyone else. As much as I respected her marriage and her first love, it had ended over three years ago. That was enough time for her to move on and fall in love with me. I suspected the she did love me but she wouldn't admit it.

Sadie and Ethan hadn't agreed upon a wedding day. I wasn't sure what they planned to do. I knew neither one of them had a lot of money, and my dad was always tight on cash. I wanted to offer to help but I had been saving my money for Elisa. If our relationship moved forward like I hoped it did, I would have a whole family to support. I saved my nickels and dimes for the occasion.

Elisa hadn't introduced me to her friends or her other brothers. I wasn't sure if she had friends but I assumed she had at least one. And I didn't know why she didn't introduce me to her family. I already knew Ethan but I wanted to know them all. I would introduce Elisa to my father in a heartbeat if I knew she was ready for it.

I got along with her kids perfectly. They were sweet and easy to handle. Tommy accidently called me dad once when Elisa wasn't around. I corrected him and told him to never do that again. I was flattered and honored with the title, but I knew it didn't belong to me. I also knew it would break Elisa's heart. As much as I wanted to be a father to those kids, I would never take that away from their real father. It wasn't his fault that he wasn't there anymore. It was just a horrific tragedy.

I still hadn't seen Elisa naked and I really wanted to see her bare skin. Whenever she bent over in front of me, I imagined what her ass looked like. I really wasn't as perverted as I seemed, but I was really hot for Elisa. Also, I hadn't ever gone that long without having sex. She and I fooled around but the intimacy wasn't the same. I wanted all of her, not just a part of her.

I knew if we had sex that would be it. We would be together, committed to one another for the long haul. I could tell her how much I loved her and come over whenever I wanted to. I could even watch the kids by myself if I wished. Everything would change once I was inside of her, and I was anxious for it to happen. I wanted Elisa for my whole life. I was ready to give myself to her.

When I came home from the gym one afternoon, I looked at my body in the mirror. I had grown in size and was covered with prominent muscles. I wasn't as big as I wanted to be but I was a good size. I knew my naked body turned Elisa on because she always wanted to see it even though she never revealed an inch of her tantalizing skin.

After I showered, I sat on the couch and watched a game on the television. I wanted to call Elisa but I didn't want to bug her too much. That's another reason why I wanted to sleep together. I wouldn't have to play it cool anymore. I could do what I wanted, when I wanted to do it, and she would have to put up with it. When my phone rang, I answered it.

"Hey, gorgeous."

"Hello, Greek god."

"I like it."

"Do you have plans tonight?"

"Plans with you."

"Can I come over?"

"You are always welcome over here, Elisa."

"I know. Can you come get me?"

"Yeah. Ethan and Sadie have the kids?"

"They are going to the movies then to Funworks."

"That sounds like fun."

"You wanna go too?"

"That's a tough decision," I said. "But I think I would rather be with you."

"You gave the right answer."

"Phew. I'm glad I didn't blow my handy."

She laughed. "Come get me."

"I'm leaving now." I hung up then walked out the door.

When I picked her up, she was wearing a long coat and heeled boots. Her hair was volumized and voluptuous. She looked amazing.

"You look great," I said.

She wrapped her arms around my neck and kissed me. "You look great too."

I grabbed her hand then guided her up the sidewalk. I was excited to spend the evening with her. Now that we had been dating for a while, we liked to lay around and watch television a lot. We didn't go out on the town or try to be hip. We were homebodies.

When we got into the apartment, I removed her coat and hung it up on the rack. When I looked at her, I immediately felt my cock get hard. She was wearing a tight black dress that fit around her curves. Her waist was tiny, very petite, and she had lovely round hips. Her thick legs had noticeable calf muscles, and her thighs were tight. Her breasts were large and round. I felt my mouth go dry at the sight of her. This was the closest I'd ever been to seeing her naked. Her skin was covered but I could see all the lines and contours. She had a smoking body.

She smiled at me while she stared at my dropped jaw. "You like it?"

"Uh—wow—yeah."

She tucked a strand of hair behind her ear while she looked at me.

"You—uh—want to go out to dinner?"

"No."

I swallowed the lump in my throat. "Then what did you want to do?"

She stepped toward me. I could hear the clap of her heels against the tile. Her hips swayed from side to side as she moved. I felt myself shake as I watched her. She placed her hands on my chest and held her lips close to mine.

I placed my hands on her back and felt her curves. My hands could span her waist, she was so small. She was perfect. My fingertips touch the beginning of her ass. I wanted to move farther down but I stopped myself from making that mistake. I didn't want to disrespect her.

"I want to go in the bedroom," she whispered.

"Uh—yeah?" I sounded like such an idiot but I couldn't stop it.

She moaned. "Yeah." She kissed my lips gently then darted her tongue into my mouth. I moaned as I felt the heat from her mouth. I pulled her tight against me so she could feel my massive erection against her hip. Suddenly, she pulled away and walked to my bedroom.

Paralyzed by her gorgeous ass, I watched her walk away. Her hips moved from side to side and her ass looked so round and firm. After she closed the door, I snapped out of my trance and followed her inside.

She was already sitting on the bed, her heels kicked off. Her dress was pulled up, showing the top of her thighs. I wanted to see more. I came to her then kneeled before her on the bed. She stared at me for a moment.

I pulled her against my chest and started to kiss her neck, tasting the sweetness of her skin. I moved my lips to her ear then back down again. She moaned quietly as I kissed her. Then she pulled my jacket off then lifted my shirt over my head. She stared at my chest with a hungry expression, feeling the muscles with her fingertips. Then she unbuttoned my pants and pulled them off, taking the underwear with her. I was completely naked before her, and she reached down and grabbed my cock, massaging me gently.

"You want to see me naked, Jared?"

My breathing was growing heavy. I stared at her chest. "Yeah."

"I thought you might."

I moaned.

She released me then placed her hands on my chest. "I want you to make love to me, Jared."

I stared into her eyes and saw the sincerity in them. She had thought about this for a while. This was exactly what I wanted. I wanted to be with her forever, commit to her in an intimate way. I wanted to show her how much I loved her. "Are you sure?"

She nodded.

I grabbed her hands and kissed them. I noticed that her wedding ring was missing. I stiffened as I realized it. She really was ready. It was she and I now.

I rose to my feet then leaned over her, pressing my body against her. She trailed her nails down my back then through my hair, looking into my eyes the entire time. I slipped my hand behind her back and pulled down the zipper all the way. When it was loose enough, I pulled it from her body.

She wore a black bra and matching thong. She had a large chest with perky tits. They were beautiful. I wrapped my hand around her neck then trailed it over her breasts then down to her thong. When I reached the fabric, I started to pull it down. "I've wanted to make love to you for so long."

"Me too."

I tossed them on the ground then looked at her. She was beautiful. I leaned down and lightly kissed the skin between her legs. She moaned.

I climbed back on top of her then unclasped her bra, pulling it free. "Elisa, you're truly gorgeous."

She grabbed my shoulders and pulled me closer to her. When I felt my naked body on top of hers, excitement coursed through me. I was so happy that this was really happening. Elisa was giving herself to me.

"It's you and me now," I whispered.

"And our children."

I felt my heart tug. "Yeah." I separated her legs then leaned over her. Before I inserted myself, I rubbed her clit and made her pant for me. I was ready to go but I wanted to make her soaked. When she gripped my forearms, I knew she was on the verge.

"Come on, Jared. I want you."

"I want you too." I kissed her forehead. "You have no idea how much." I opened my nightstand drawer and pulled out a condom.

She steadied my hand. "I don't want to use one."

"You want to have another baby?" I asked with a smile. "I'm okay with that."

"I'm on birth control, and I'm clean. I hope you are too."

I tossed the packet aside. "I've never had sex without one."

"You're going to love it," she said as she scratched my back.

"I may not last long."

"That's okay."

I grabbed her face and kissed her, leaning far over her. I reached my hands out and grabbed hers, squeezing them in mine. I pressed my forehead against hers. "I love you, Ellie." I inserted myself within her and immediately felt her stretch.

"Oh—uh," she said with a breath.

I continued to look at her as I felt her intimately. She was wet and smooth. Her tender flesh moved across my tip and made me shake. I never felt direct skin before and it was amazing. I could feel every inch of her. "Ellie."

She squeezed my hands as she rocked me from below. "Jared."

"God," I said as I thrust inside her gently. "You feel amazing."

She leaned up and kissed me gently, lightly pressing her tongue against mine. The pleasure was driving me wild. I already wanted to come but I held it back. I wanted to make this moment perfect for her.

I increased my pace slightly to make her climax. I wanted to give her the best orgasm she ever had. I removed one hand and started to rub her clitoris, combining both sites to make a massive explosion. I knew it was working because she started to moan uncontrollably.

"Jared," she said with a moan. "Jared."

"Come for me."

"Oh my god."

"That's it."

She scratched her nails down my back and opened her legs wider, using her hips to move inside me faster. "Yes, yes."

I kissed her neck as she rode her explosion, holding her tightly through the wave of her pleasure. When she was done, she caught her breath for a moment.

"Oh god," she said.

I couldn't hold on much longer. When I thought about how beautiful she looked, I felt my mind snap. The orgasm pounded through me and set me off. "I've never come inside someone before."

"I want you to."

"Yeah," I said as I thrust inside her harder. It rocked through me and left me feeling faint. It was a unique feeling. Elisa made me come when she jerked me but it felt nothing like this. Everything was different now. She and I were really together. She chose me.

I kissed her gently before I pulled out. When I rolled on my back, she climbed on top of me.

"Oh my fucking god." Her face was stretched in a smile and her eyes were bright.

"What?" I asked with a smile.

"That was so amazing!"

"Well, I try," I said with shrug.

"You're really good at that. I want to do it all the time."

"Deal," I said with a laugh. I knew I was good in bed but I didn't think I was as amazing as she made it sound. But then I remembered she hadn't had sex in three years. That was a long time not to get laid. It wasn't surprising that it was wonderful to her. "I'm glad you enjoyed it."

"Enjoyed it?" she said incredulously. "My god, you're hot, Jared. Damn hot."

"You're just making me blush now."

"Your cock is so big."

"Well, yeah." I wondered if I was bigger than her husband. I must be if she said that. I tried not to think about it. I didn't want to be compared.

She leaned down and kissed my chest everywhere. "You taste good too."

"That was the best sex I've ever had."

She raised an eyebrow. "Really?"

"I've never made love to someone that I was in love with. It was amazing to me too."

"You're so sweet, Jared."

"For you I am."

"I'm glad."

"Now you're mine," I said as I stared her down, daring her to challenge me.

"I know."

"You're all mine, every inch of you."

"I want to be yours."

"Good."

She lay on top of my chest and closed her eyes. "You're so warm."

"It's my job to keep you warm."

"You're doing a great job."

"Sleep with me tonight."

"And go home in the morning?"

"Yeah. I want you to sleep with me every night."

"But what about the kids?"

"I'll take you home before they wake up."

"But we can't sleep together every night."

"I can sleep over there."

She was quiet for a moment. "I suppose."

"I want the kids to get uscd to seeing me every morning. We sleep together and we're together. I love their mommy. They'll understand it eventually."

She said nothing.

"Is that okay, Ellie?"

"Yes."

"I realize it's a big commitment, but I want to do it."

"I do too."

I breathed a sigh of relief. "That's what I was hoping for."

She cuddled next to me and closed her eyes.

I leaned over and set the alarm then held her to my chest, protecting her in my arms. When her breathing grew light, I knew she was asleep. I ran my fingers through her hair for a long time before I finally fell into darkness.

# 8

When I took Elisa home in the morning, I gave her a long kiss before I left. "I'll see you when I get off work."

"Ethan and I have some errands to run tonight."

"I'll take you."

"You will?"

"Don't ask Ethan anymore. I'll take you—I want to take you."

She smiled.

"What do you need to get?"

"Groceries and some other things."

"I'll head over as soon as I'm off."

"Okay."

"I'll see you later." I turned away and let her close the door. After I heard her lock it, I waved down a cab and headed to work. It was a pretty uneventful day. I sat in my office and responded to all the emails I had. Then I got to work on all the big stuff.

Around lunchtime, Ethan came into my office. "Hey."

"Hey," I said.

"So, where were you guys last night?"

I looked at him. "At my apartment."

"All night?"

I rose from my chair then shut the door. When I returned to my seat, I glared at him. "I respect the fact that you protect your sister and look after her, but when you gave me permission to date her, you also gave me your trust. I will take care of her. Don't worry about it."

"You didn't answer my question."

"Yes, she and I were at my apartment all night. I dropped her off before I went to work."

"So this is serious now?"

"It's been serious."

"You're not messing with her?"

"You're starting to piss me off. I love your sister, I want to marry your sister, and I want to adopt her kids. If all I wanted was sleep with her, I wouldn't have stuck around so long. She and I are happy together. And to be frank, I'm sick of this older brother act. Knock it off. I mean it."

He stared at me but said nothing.

"If I ever hurt your sister, then you can hunt me down. But don't accuse me of anything until that actually happens."

"My job is to prevent it from happening."

I sighed. "I don't know what more I can say. I told you the truth. I love her and I want to be with her."

"You're not getting cold feet?"

"My feet are on fire."

He stared at me.

"I'm sick of this bullshit. If that's all you have to say to me, then don't speak to me at all."

He sighed. "You're right. I'm sorry. I—I'm just not handling this well."

I leaned back in my chair and looked at him. "What do you mean?"

"I'm assuming that you slept together since she stayed there all night?"

I said nothing.

"Don't answer that. If that's what happened, that means she's really moving on. You're going to be staying at the house, taking care of the kids, and then she isn't going to need me anymore. She'll have you."

I was quiet for a moment. "Isn't that a good thing?"

"Yes, of course. But—I don't know. It's just hard for me to accept. I'm used to being the man in her life, the guardian to her kids."

Now I understood his meaning. "That isn't going to change, Ethan."

"Yes, it is."

"Elisa still wants you to be around all the time. And frankly, I do too. It's nice having a stand by babysitter."

He laughed. "I guess."

"I'm not trying to replace you."

"I know."

"Your sister is in good hands."

He nodded. "I know that too."

"And you don't need to jump ahead so quickly. I'm not going to move in right away and kick you out. We'll take it slow. I want the kids to be comfortable with me before we make huge changes."

"Thanks."

"Yeah."

"So you guys are going to move in together?"

"Uh—I don't know. We haven't talked about it. I'm not sure how she would feel about that since we aren't married."

"I don't know either."

"I would like to get married but I don't think she's ready for that yet."

"And you are?"

I was quiet for a moment. "Yeah, I think so."

Ethan rubbed his palms together. "Well, don't rush into anything unless you are sure."

"Yeah."

"You make her happy. Keep it up.

"Really?"

"Yeah. I know she really likes you. I haven't seen her this happy in a long time. She started to sing again."

"She sings?"

"Like an angel."

"I didn't know that."

"Well, now you do."

"I'm glad that I make her so happy."

"I am too."

"So, we're cool?"

He smiled. "Yeah. Sorry I was being a jackass before."

"You mean a crazy asshole?"

"So you heard me and Sadie argue?"

"It's an appropriate nickname."

He laughed. "Yeah. It's perfect," he said sarcastically. "I forgot to mention something. Elisa's birthday is this week. I wasn't sure if you knew that."

"No," I said quickly. "Thanks for telling me."

"Yeah. She's pretty quiet about it. I figured she didn't tell you."

"When is it?"

"Thursday."

"Thanks."

"I guess I'll see you later."

"Oh. Elisa said she needed to go to the store today. I offered to take her."

He nodded. "That's cool."

I knew he felt like I was stepping on his toes so I added, "You can still come. I just wanted to try and save you from the ordeal."

He laughed. "No. I need to get some things anyway."

"Cool."

"I'll see you later." He left the office, leaving the door open.

When the day was finally over, Ethan and I took a cab back to the townhouse on the other side of town. Now that we had our talk, it didn't feel so awkward anymore. He was marrying my sister and I accepted that. I knew he would take care of her. Initially, I was worried that he was still the dog he used to be, but he clearly wasn't. And he seemed to accept my love for Elisa. Obviously, there were feelings below the surface in that respect.

When we walked inside, Elisa rose to her feet and greeted me with a big kiss. I melted in her arms and felt my heart accelerate. I wanted her to greet me that way every day. I imagined coming home to her, my wife, and seeing my kids while she cooked dinner in the kitchen. This was exactly what I wanted.

"How was your day?" she asked.

"Good," I said. "Glad it's over."

"Me too," she said.

"So are you ready to go shopping?"

"Yes," she said.

Sadie came down the hall and smiled at me. "Where are you going?"

"We need to get groceries," I answered.

"Well, I'll watch the kids while you're gone."

"Thanks," I said. "Ready to go, Ellie?"

"Yeah," she said as she grabbed her purse.

The three of us walked out the door then headed to the market up the street. I kept my arm around Elisa the entire way and held her close to me. A few shady people walked by and she moved even closer to me. I hated seeing her scared of everyone and everything. I knew that's why she never went anywhere alone and locked the door so many times.

When we entered the grocery store, Elisa grabbed a cart and started walking down the aisles. Ethan and I trailed behind her until we saw the new video game console on display in front of the story. Elisa continued her grocery shopping while we acted like teenage boys.

"Dude, we should get it," Ethan said.

"I know. But we'll just end up playing it the whole time."

"Too bad the kids aren't older. We could use them as an excuse."

I laughed. "Yeah."

I looked over my shoulder to check on Elisa and saw her talking to some guy. He was standing very close to her and she kept stepping back, clearly uncomfortable. The sight made my mind snap. I marched over to them then stepped in front of her, blocking her from view. "Can I help you with something?"

He glared at me. "No, but you can get out of my way."

"Back off."

"I'm just talking to this beautiful lady."

I stepped closer to him. He was the same height as me but not nearly as muscular. I saw him flinch as I approached him. "Leave my girlfriend alone."

He glared at me before he backed off and walked down the aisle.

When I turned back to Elisa, she looked relieved.

"Thanks," she whispered.

I wrapped my arm around her and kissed her forehead. "You never have to be scared when you're with me."

She rested her face against my chest. "I know."

"Do you have pepper spray or a tazer?"

She looked scared. "No."

"Do you want one?"

"Do you think I need it?" She sounded frightened.

"No, you'll never need one as long as I'm around, but if it makes you feel better, I'll get you one."

She shook her head. "No. I don't want one."

I was quiet for a moment. "Okay."

"Just don't leave me."

"I'm so sorry. I forget how beautiful you are. People must bother you all the time."

She said nothing.

Now I felt like an idiot. I should have figured it out before. What was the point of being so gorgeous when people bothered you all the time? It was a curse, not a blessing. "It won't happen again."

"It's not your fault, Jared."

"Yes, it is," I said sadly. "Come on. Let's finish that list."

"Okay." She started to push the cart but I got behind it and guided it for her. She smiled at me then grabbed her items. I trailed behind her and just watched her shop. A few men stared at her, but when they caught my look they looked away.

When we were done, we went to the checkout counter and met Ethan. He was about to combine his items with hers so he could pay for it, but I stopped him. "I got it."

He raised an eyebrow. "You're sure?"

"Don't worry about it."

Elisa looked at me. "You don't have to do that, Jared."

"I take care of you now," I said. "I don't mind."

Elisa fell quiet.

I grabbed her face and kissed her. "I want to take care of you."

She smiled at me. "You're so sweet, Jared."

I paid for the groceries then grabbed the bags. I didn't let her carry anything. When Ethan was done, we left the store. I noticed he only had one bag. "What did you get?"

He said nothing for a moment. He grabbed the box and showed it to us.

"Tampons?" I asked with disgust.

He shrugged. "Sadie asked me to get some."

Elisa smiled. "Tom used to do it for me all the time."

"Yeah, but that's different."

"How?" she asked.

"It just is," he said.

"Are you sure you want to get married?" I asked.

"I'm having second thoughts," he said with a laugh.

"It's not too late," I said.

"Stop being jerks," Elisa said. She looked at me. "You would do it if I asked you to."

I smiled at her. "Well, that's different. I would do anything for you."

She smiled at me and Ethan rolled his eyes.

When we got home, I helped Elisa put all the groceries away while everyone stayed in the living room. When we were done, I looked at her. "I'm really sorry about today. It won't happen again."

"Jared, you didn't do anything wrong. When you saw someone bothering me, you took care of it."

"It shouldn't have happened at all."

"He didn't try to hurt me."

"That's beside the point." I grabbed her face and looked at her. "You never have to worry about your safety with me. I want you to know that."

"I believe you, Jared."

"I can go to the store for you if you're more comfortable with that."

She sighed. "As much as I would love that, I can't stay in the house forever."

I kissed her nose. "Let me know if you change your mind."

"Okay," she said. "And Jared?"

"Yeah?"

"I know you can take care of me."

I smiled. "That means the world to me."

We moved into the living room and sat on the couch. I played with Tommy for a while then read him a story. Becky crawled into Elisa's lap and started to color in her coloring book. Ethan and Sadie sat on the couch tangled up together. Ethan drank from his beer while he played with Sadie's hair.

As much as I enjoyed spending time with Elisa as a family, I wanted to go to bed and make love to her. It'd been on my mind since the first time we did it. I felt awkward that Ethan was in the next room, but I didn't care enough to not pursue it.

When Tommy finally fell asleep in my lap, I smiled. Ethan and Sadie retired to bed and we put the kids to sleep in their rooms. I didn't want to be presumptuous with Elisa by assuming we were going to bed so I waited for her to initiate it.

"So, are you ready to go to sleep?"

"No, but I'm ready for bed," I said with smile. "Are you still okay with me sleeping here?"

"Yeah. Let's go."

We went into her bedroom and closed the door behind us. The bedspread was white with purple pillows. The rug on the floor was also purple. The room was littered with picture frames of her kids. She had a private bathroom and a walk in closet. It was nice of Ethan to give her the better room even though he was paying the rent. I stepped toward the bed and saw the picture frame on her nightstand.

It was a man with brown hair. I knew that was her husband. When she caught my look, she walked over and turned it over, face down.

I stood next to her then grabbed the picture, returning it to its position.

She held a look of surprise.

"I told you when we got together that I understood that you still loved your husband. You don't have to hide him from me. I would never want you to."

Tears bubbled in her eyes.

"And I certainly don't want you to forget about him."

She wiped her tear away. "I don't know what to say."

"I said I would settle for a part of your heart. I know you can't give me the whole thing."

She said nothing.

"Leave this picture here."

Elisa nodded. "You're the sweetest guy, Jared."

"No. I'm just in love with you. I want to make you happy, not cause you pain. You can love both of us. I'm okay with that."

"I don't want to forget about him," she whispered.

"Good." I kissed her on the forehead then started to strip my clothes away.

Her tears disappeared as she watched me remove my shirt and pants. I recognized the look in her eyes. I knew she wanted me. When I pulled down my briefs, she stared at my cock. I was hard but I was always hard around her. I walked over to her then pulled her shirt from her body. She lifted her arms and let me remove it.

Elisa placed her hands on my chest then felt my body. She stared at me hungrily while she felt all my muscles. The longing in her eyes made me feel aroused. I liked knowing I made her feel that way. I grabbed her pants and pulled them down then removed her underwear.

As I held her face and kissed her, I guided her toward the bed and laid her down. She immediately wrapped her legs around my waist and pulled me toward her.

"Jared," she whispered. "I want you."

"I know," I said as I kissed her everywhere. I placed my cock against her stomach and let my juice drip on her. She grabbed me and started to stroke me. I continued to kiss her while I played with her nipples, making her even hotter.

She was panting for me. "I want you inside me. Please."

"You want it?"

"I'll beg if I have to."

I pulled her hips toward me then slid inside her.

She moaned happily as I stretched her. "Yeah, Jared."

I moved hard and fast.

She bit her lip as she rocked her hips from below.

I thrust into her faster.

"I can't believe it," she whispered. "I'm already coming."

"Ellie."

She grabbed my shoulders as she thrust into me harder. "Oh—god."

She was getting too loud so I covered her lips with my own and silenced her words with my kiss. Her breathing had increased and she gripped me even tighter. When she released her grip, I knew she was finished. I broke our kiss then sat back on my heels, bucking myself inside of her hard. Within a few seconds, I was coming.

I moaned but kept quiet. "Ellie."

"Jared."

I emptied myself entirely. I kissed her then pulled out of her.

"I want to do it again."

I smiled. "We can do it as many times as you want."

"Good," she said as she snuggled next to me.

"You can pick the position next time."

"Ooh. I look forward to it."

I kissed her on the forehead then fell asleep.

# 9

At first, the kids were confused by my appearance in the morning. When I had breakfast with them at the table, they stared at me and asked me questions.

"Do you live here now too?" Tommy asked.

"No. But I'll be here a lot."

"Do you like my mommy?"

I smiled. "I like her a lot."

Becky made a disgusted face. "Eww. You don't want to like her."

"Why?" I asked.

"She can be mean."

I laughed. "How?"

"She gets mad when I don't put my toys away," she said as she poked her eggs.

"Good," I said. "You should put your toys away."

She made a disgusted face at me. I wasn't going to win their support by playing the good cop and making Elisa the bad cop. I intended to be a good guardian and role model, even if they didn't like me all the time. I would discipline them and call them out when they were wrong. I didn't know much about kids but I knew I had to be consistent with them.

When Elisa listened to me speak to the children, I knew she was pleased. I always took equal responsibility for punishments. I made it clear that she and I were a team and agreed on every decision. They couldn't run to me when they wanted to get away with something.

As the days went by, they didn't question my appearance. They expected me to be there every morning, and when I wasn't, they asked about me. It was cramped in the morning when we all got ready for the day. We had four adults, two kids, and one dog in the house. Koku was happy with the arrangement. He always had someone to pay attention to him. In fact, he tried to get away from us for some quiet time when he could. I still paid rent on my apartment even though I was hardly ever there. I wanted to move in permanently but I wasn't sure if she was ready for that.

When we were eating breakfast one morning, I looked at her. "You wanna go out to dinner tonight?"

"Yeah, sure," she said as she ate her omelet. One of the good things about being there all the time was the home cooked meals.

"Is it okay if my dad is there?" I tried to slide that in casually.

She stopped eating. "Uh—just us and your dad?"

"Yeah," I said. "Just a casual dinner."

"You want me to meet him?"

"Of course. Why wouldn't I?"

"Uh, okay."

"Don't be scared, Ellie."

"I'm not," she said quietly. I knew she was lying. I wasn't sure if it was because she was nervous or she just wasn't ready. I gave her a quick kiss before I left for work. I hadn't even asked my dad if he wanted to have dinner so I decided to go by the shop on my break.

"Look who it is," he said happily as I walked in.

"Hey, pops."

"What brings you here?"

"I was wondering if you had plans tonight?"

"Just with the television."

Sadie emerged from the back and smiled at me. "Hey."

"Hey," I said to her. I turned back to my dad. "So, you wanna come to dinner with me and Elisa?"

"I'm finally going to meet the woman who's made an honest man out of my son?"

I smiled. "It seems so."

"Sure. I would love to. Is she bringing the kids?"

"No. They'll be with Ethan."

"Do I get to meet them too?" he asked hopefully.

"Next time," I said.

"Great. I'll see you tonight," he said. He picked up a box and walked into the back.

"That's exciting," Sadie said. "You're really moving forward."

"We've been moving forward."

She smiled. "I'm very happy for you."

"Thank you."

"So, are you going to ask soon?"

"How did you know?"

"You seemed to be in a rush to introduce her to Dad, and you practically live at the house."

"I want to move in but I think she would feel more comfortable if we were married. She wouldn't bring someone around the kids if they weren't going to stick around."

"That makes sense," she said. "So when?"

"As soon as she's ready."

"Do you think she is?"

"She might be. She agreed to meet Dad."

"That's true."

I looked at my watch. "I have to get back to work. I'll see you later."

"Bye."

I finished my work day then headed to the gym before I went to Elisa's. I started taking a boxing and self-defense class at the gym. I knew how to fight but I wanted to brush up on my skills. I wasn't frightened of something happening to me, but I wanted to prove that I could take care of Elisa. I knew it would make her feel better if I was educated in fighting skills.

When I arrived at the house, Elisa seemed nervous. She wore a tight dark blue dress and her hair was done. She looked beautiful like she always did.

"You look lovely," I said as I kissed her. Her lips barely moved when they touched mine. I tried to act like I didn't notice. If I gave her a chance to voice her doubts, she may not come along. "You ready?"

"Yeah," she said with a nod.

"Great." I grabbed her hand and led her out the door. We walked down the street until I waved down a cab. I helped her get inside before I sat beside her. "You'll never guess what happened at work today."

"What?" she asked with a quiet voice.

"One of my colleagues placed a whoopee cushion in my boss' seat. Yeah…he didn't like that very much."

She stared laughing and the color returned to her cheeks. "I never expected that from a room full of suits."

"Ethan knows who it is."

"He does?"

"Yeah, but he won't tell me, that jerk."

"He's probably trying to protect the transgressor."

"Well, he can tell me. I'm almost his brother."

"In law."

"When you mix blood with water, it still looks like blood."

She stared at me for a moment then looked away.

I wrapped my arm around her shoulder and leaned close to her. "Tell me about your day." I wanted to get her mind off dinner. When she thought about other things, she didn't seem so nervous.

"The kids and I did some crafts."

"Such as?"

"We made snowflakes."

"That sounds pretty cool."

She smiled. "Tommy's looked like it came out of the shredder and Becky painted hers pink."

"That's even better. They are being creative."

She laughed. "I suppose."

"Remember Picasso? Everyone thought that guy was crazy and he turned out to be one of the greatest artists ever."

"Are you comparing my son to Picasso?"

"In a good way," I said quickly.

"Well, I'm glad you think my son is crazy," she said with a laugh.

"No. He's eccentric."

"That sounds equally bad."

The cab stopped and I paid the driver then stepped out. I helped her get out then walked toward the entrance. I could feel the tension in her hand. I stopped and looked at her. "Ellie, it doesn't make a difference whether he likes you or not. Please don't be nervous. And I can guarantee that he'll like you anyway."

She tucked a strand of hair behind her ear but said nothing.

"Come on." We walked inside then spotted my dad at a table by the window. We moved toward him as he rose to stand.

"Elisa!" he said happily. "It's very wonderful to meet you." He grabbed her and hugged her tightly.

She smiled as she pulled away. "It's nice to meet you, Mr. Montague."

He waved a hand. "Don't call me that. Bill is fine."

"Then why does Ethan call you that?" I asked.

My dad sat down. "That's different."

I pulled out Elisa's chair and helped her take a seat. I sat next to her and put my arm around her.

"So my son is a little hung up on you," my dad said.

"Thanks for being so cool about it, Dad," I said sarcastically.

Elisa smiled. "I like him too—most of the time."

My dad laughed. "I like her already."

I looked at her, silently telling her I was right.

"So how are the kids?" he asked.

"Great," she said. "They are both wonderful."

"Do you have any pictures?" he asked excitedly.

"Uh, yeah." She pulled out her phone then handed it to him.

"Awe. They are adorable," my dad said. "What are their names?"

"Tommy and Becky."

My dad nodded. "Good names."

"Becky was the name of my mother, and Tommy was the name of my husband." She averted her gaze when she said this. I rubbed her shoulder to dispel the concern that she felt.

"My son told me what happened. I'm very sorry."

"Thank you," she said quietly.

Now I wanted to change the subject. "How's the shop, Dad?"

"It's the same, really. It's been slow."

I nodded. "Maybe you should start selling porn and cigarettes."

He rolled his eyes. "Jared has wanted me to do that since he hit puberty."

I shrugged. "It would work. I'm tellin' ya."

"You would be my only customer," he said with a laugh.

"Some business is better than no business," I said.

My dad looked at Elisa. "Get out while you can."

She laughed.

My dad pointed at her. "She's a keeper."

I kissed her on the cheek. "I know she is."

She looked at me with flushed cheeks.

The waiter came over and took our order. We talked about Sadie's wedding for a long time.

"Did she decide to invite her mother?" my father asked.

"I don't know."

"Well, she should."

"It's her day, Dad. She can invite whoever she wants."

"It's her mother," he argued.

"What does that matter? She took off without looking back. I don't want her there either."

He sighed. "The last thing I want is for my kids to hate their mother."

"We don't hate her," I corrected. "We just don't care for her. I haven't seen her in seven years. She hasn't come to visit us once. Even if we did invite her to the wedding, she probably wouldn't come anyway."

"It's always nice to be invited."

"Dad, I really don't think she's going to change her mind. Ethan is persuasive but he isn't a magician."

He sighed. "That makes me very sad."

"Just let it go."

"So she hasn't picked a date yet? A venue?"

"No. They'll probably just do it at city hall."

"Why?"

"Well, they don't have money for anything big."

"Doesn't Ethan work with you?"

"Yeah, but—he's got student loans." I didn't want to reveal that he took care of Elisa. I assumed she didn't want him to know either.

The waiter brought our food and we began to eat quietly. Elisa ate like a goddess. She had perfect grace and poise.

My dad looked at Elisa. "I would love to meet your children. They are always welcome at my house if you ever want to come visit. Or just need a babysitter so you can have the night off."

"Thank you. That's very sweet."

I smiled at my dad. I appreciated all the support he was giving me. He knew I really liked Elisa. I had never introduced him to a girl before so he knew I was serious about her. When we were finished, I paid the bill then we left the restaurant. We said our goodbyes on the curb.

"It was nice to meet you," my dad said as he hugged Elisa. "Please don't be a stranger."

"Thank you," she said with a smile.

I hugged my dad next.

"Good job," he said as he patted my back.

"Thanks." I knew what he meant. "I'll see you later."

We walked to a cab then drove back to the townhouse down the road. Elisa was quiet on the drive.

"That wasn't so bad, right?" I asked.

"He was very sweet," she said with a smile.

"Yeah. My dad is a badass."

She laughed. "Well, I wouldn't say that."

"He's a cool guy. I like him a lot."

"I liked him too."

"And I know he liked you—a lot."

"It seemed that way," she said quietly.

"What's bothering you?" I asked her blatantly.

"Nothing," she said quickly. "I liked your dad. He was cute."

I stared at her for a moment then dropped the conversation. Perhaps she was still nervous after the meeting. I thought it went well. My dad loved her and she liked him. He even wanted to meet her kids. If that wasn't a declaration of his approval, then I didn't know what was.

When we got home, the kids were already asleep.

"Hey," I said as I put my coat on the rack.

"Hey," Sadie said. "How'd it go?"

"It went great," I said. "Dad loves her."

Ethan looked at Elisa. "Had a good time?"

"Yeah," she said.

We sat on the couch and I pulled her close to me.

"Did he ask about Mom?" Sadie asked.

"Yeah," I answered. "He thinks you should still invite her."

"Nope," she said.

Ethan shrugged. "I tried."

"He doesn't want us to hate her," I added.

"I don't hate her," Sadie said. "I just don't like her."

I laughed. "I said the same thing."

Sadie looked Elisa. "Was my father sweet to you?"

"He was very nice to me," she answered.

"He's wanted to meet you for a while," Sadie said.

"Oh?" Elisa said.

"Yeah. You're the first girl Jared has brought around."

She stared at me for a moment. "I didn't know that."

I met her gaze. "It's true." I kissed her on the forehead then the cheek. "I'm a bit obsessed with you, really."

She said nothing.

"Baby, let's go to bed," Ethan said as he picked her up.

"That was sudden," Sadie said as he lifted her.

"Well, I'm tired," he said as he carried her down the hall. Koku emerged from the kitchen and followed behind them.

I rubbed my nose against Elisa's. "Ready for bed, Ellie?"

She nodded.

I rose from the couch then walked into her bedroom with her trailing behind me. When we closed the door, I started to strip off my clothes. When my clothes were off she was practically salivating.

She turned away and started to undress herself. I came up behind her and pressed my naked body against her then I kissed her neck, gliding my tongue down the skin. I grabbed her hips and pressed her ass against my cock. I knew she could feel it. She was responsive but not as much as normally.

I pulled up her dress and pressed my dick against her skin. Then I reached down and started to rub her in the way that she liked. In a moment, she was breathing heavily for me, moaning like usual.

I unzipped her dress, letting it drop to the floor, then removed her thong. I pushed her against the wall, my chest against her back. The dynamic between us was completely different. Whatever was bothering her had left her mind. Now she wanted me to fuck her.

"How do you want it, Ellie?"

"Like this," she said with a moan.

"I was hoping you would say that." I dragged her to the bed then pushed her down, pulling her ass to me. The sight of her bent over made me want to explode. I enjoyed making love but I also enjoyed fucking her like crazy.

I pressed my tip against her entrance and I felt the moisture. I could slip inside so easily. "You're so wet, baby."

She moaned.

With a single thrust, I was inside her. I still wasn't used to having sex without condoms so the feel of her bare flesh was always a shock. It was so slippery and smooth. "Fuck," I whispered.

"Jared." She grabbed my arm and pulled me further into her.

"Damn." I pressed my chest against her back. It was smooth and warm. I slowly thrust inside of her while I rubbed her clit. "Try to be quiet."

"I—I can't," she said as she bit her lip.

I continued to move inside her. "The quieter you are, the harder I go."

"Oh god."

I slowed down.

She fell silent.

"Good girl," I said as I increased my pace.

She reached behind her and grabbed my ass, pulling me into her. I was careful not to rock the bed too much. Her breathing had increased and she was practically hyperventilating.

"Stay quiet," I whispered.

She moaned.

I slowed down.

"Please," she whispered.

I moved even slower.

She grabbed my ass and squeezed.

I bucked inside of her hard, inserting myself as far as I would go. She stayed quiet and I was astounded. I continued to move inside her, loving every inch of her. "God, I love you."

Her orgasm kicked in and she was doing a horrible job of staying quiet. Since she was already coming, I didn't slow down because I wanted to make her feel good. She whispered my name over and over, which made me come at the same time.

"Ellie," I whispered. "God." Now I couldn't stay quiet.

When we were both finished, I kissed her spine until I reached her neck. Then I massaged her skin, making her relax. She lay down and with me beside her.

She patted my chest. "You did good."

I laughed. "Thanks. I'm glad I satisfy you."

She cuddled next to me and rested her head on my chest. "That was fun."

"It was," I said as I kissed her forehead. "Since tomorrow is a special day, I was hoping I could take you out."

She looked at me. "What's tomorrow?"

"Your birthday."

"Ethan told you?"

"Yep."

She sighed.

"Have dinner with me."

"Okay," she said with a smile. "No gifts."

"Okay."

"I know you're lying."

I shrugged. "Maybe."

She closed her eyes then fell asleep. I stared at her for a long time before I was able to follow behind her.

# 10

I woke up early the next morning and got the kids ready then placed them at the kitchen table. I cooked breakfast—tried to cook breakfast—and waited for my beautiful woman to wake up. When she came into the kitchen, her face broke into a smile.

"What's this?" she asked.

I looked at the kids. "That's your cue."

"Happy birthday!" they squealed. They both held up the paintings they made for her, under my supervision, and waved them at her. Tommy's painting looked like a black smudge and Becky's looked like bubblegum.

Elisa had tears in her eyes as she looked at her kids. "You made these for me?"

Tommy handed it to her. "This is you."

She looked at it with a smile. "It's wonderful, dear."

"Look at mine!" Becky yelled.

Elisa looked at it.

"It's you as a princess, Mommy!"

"I can see that," she lied. "It's beautiful. Thank you so much." She kissed each of them on the head then hugged them tightly. There were tears in her eyes and she tried to blink them away.

I turned off the stove then walked over to her. "Happy birthday, honey."

She smiled at me. "You did this?"

"No. We all did it," I said as I looked at the kids. I kissed her on the forehead. "You look beautiful."

"I just woke up," she said with flushed cheeks.

"I don't understand the relevance." I pulled out a chair for her and had her sit down. "Come on." When she sat down, I pushed her chair in. "Breakfast is coming up."

I grabbed the plates then set them on the table. We started to eat together when Ethan walked into the room.

"Happy birthday, baby sister." He kissed her on the head.

"Thank you," she answered.

Ethan grabbed a plate and started to eat. "Why does this taste weird?"

"Jared cooked today," she explained.

"I *tried* to cook," I corrected.

"Oh," Ethan said. "It tastes great."

I laughed. "I know my cooking sucks in comparison to Elisa's."

"It's the thought that counts," Elisa said.

"What a pity compliment," Ethan said with a laugh.

Elisa glared at him. "It's not pity. It's incredibly sweet."

I smiled. "I'm glad you like it."

Koku came to my leg and started to beg for food. "Koku obviously think it's good."

"But he eats his own shit," Ethan said.

Elisa glared at him. "Don't cuss, Ethan."

"Damn," he said. "I mean, wait—oh forget it."

I laughed. I tried very hard not to curse around the children and I hadn't had a slip up yet.

Sadie came into the room holding a vase of flowers. "Happy birthday, Elisa," she said as she placed them in the middle of the table.

"Awe," Elisa said. "They are beautiful. Thank you."

"You're welcome." She sat down beside me and started to eat. She gave Koku a few scraps, but after he smelled it he walked away.

Ethan laughed. "That was just sad."

I shook my head. "Clearly I need more practice."

"Or you should stop—for humanity."

"Leave him alone," Elisa said. "I think it's great."

"We all know you're lying," Ethan said. "Don't bother."

She reached across the table and grabbed my hand. "Thank you."

Sadie took a bite of her food then made a face. "Wait, Jared made this?"

"Yeah," Ethan said with a laugh.

"You should have said something before," she said as she chewed.

Ethan laughed. "You're so cute, baby."

"Even when I look like I'm going to throw up?"

"Don't be annoying," I said to her. "I wanted to do something nice for the woman I love."

"And you succeeded," Elisa said to me.

Ethan stood up. "Well, I'm going to head to work—and grab breakfast on the way."

I laughed. "Something so sweet turned so laughable."

Ethan shrugged then kissed Sadie on the head. "I'll see you later, baby."

Sadie rose from the chair then dumped her plate in the sink. "I'm leaving too."

They both bolted out the door.

I looked at Elisa. "I'm sorry it isn't very good."

"It's fine, Jared. Don't listen to them."

"Okay."

I looked at my watch. "I need to get going. I'll do the dishes when I get home."

"Don't be ridiculous," she said with a laugh.

We rose from the table then walked to the front door. She wrapped her arms around my neck and kissed me. It was gentle and wet. When she pulled away, she pressed her forehead against mine. "Thank you for breakfast."

"Of course," I said. "We still on for tonight?"

"Yeah," she said with a smile.

"And you'll get your birthday sex later."

She blushed. "I better."

"Oh you will."

I gave her one last kiss before I walked out the door.

When I got to work, I had to organize all the accounts I was handling then speak to my clients. The job was rudimentary and repetitive. Sometimes I was actually bored. But it paid the bills and gave me a flashy title. I called the restaurant and made the reservations before I went home.

I grabbed the box from my bedroom then changed before I headed back to Elisa's. As I was walking there, I imagined what she would be wearing and how she looked. I knew she would be beautiful, but just how beautiful was still a mystery.

When she opened the door, my mouth dropped. She was wearing a low cut dress with a high slit, revealing her legs.

"You—look—yes."

"Thanks," she said. "You look very handsome as well."

"Well—duh."

She laughed.

"You ready?"

"Well—duh," she snapped.

I laughed then grabbed her hand. "Let's go."

We walked to the restaurant. It was a fancy Italian restaurant. I knew Elisa didn't go out very often and I wanted to do something nice for her. When we approached the table, I pulled out the chair for her and she sat down.

"This place is really nice, Jared."

"And I'm sure their cooking is better than mine."

She laughed. "It wasn't that bad."

"That bad? Koku wouldn't even eat it."

"Maybe he wasn't hungry."

"That dog is always hungry."

"It was sweet either way."

"Well, I'm glad you appreciated it. I just hope I didn't poison our kids."

She flinched after I spoke. I wondered if the use of *our* is what made her uncomfortable. It just slipped out. I wasn't thinking. Instead of making the situation worse, I decided to drop it.

"How was your day?" I asked.

"Good. I placed the paintings on the refrigerator."

"Future works of art."

"Maybe," she said with a smile.

I leaned forward. "Did I mention how beautiful you look tonight?"

She blushed. "Thank you."

"Have you thought about what kind of sex you want to have?"

She smiled. "A little."

"I'm glad you're doing some real brainstorming. People need to take birthday sex more seriously."

"It's a tough decision."

While we were eating, I looked across the room I saw my ex, Suzie, sitting across from a guy. She was clearly on a date. I hoped she wouldn't notice me, and if she did, I hoped she wouldn't talk to me. The last thing I wanted to do was make Elisa uncomfortable with a crazy ex. It wouldn't make me look good.

When we were finished, I pulled out the cash and left it on the table. "Are you ready, m'lady?"

"Yes."

I pulled out her chair and helped her stand up. I guided her out of the restaurant and avoided Suzie as much as possible. I know I broke her heart when I dumped her. But I had to do it. That bitch was crazy.

"Thank you for taking me to dinner," she said.

"Yeah, of course. Did you like your food?"

"It was great."

"Good."

We didn't say anything on the cab ride home. She placed her hand on my thigh and rubbed me gently. I started thinking about birthday sex. When we pulled in front of the house, I handed the money to the driver then got out.

Everyone was asleep when we walked inside. It wasn't late but the house was silent. We walked into the bedroom and closed the door.

"So have you decided yet?" I asked as I loosened my tie.

"Too many options," she said as she kicked off her heels.

"Well, I'll give you your gift now so you have more time."

"You got me something? You've done more than enough."

"It will never be enough for the woman I love."

Her eyes softened. I pulled the box out of my pocket then sat beside her on the bed. I was careful not to get down on one knee. "Here," I said as I handed it to her.

She took the box and opened the ribbon. "Tiffany's?" she asked. "They are so expensive."

"Ignore that."

She opened the lid and pulled out the necklace. It was a heart made of white gold. She stared at it affectionately.

"It's a locket."

She opened the clasp and looked at the picture. It was a picture of Becky and Tommy holding up the paintings they made for her. She stared at it for a long time without saying anything. Her lack of reaction frightened me. I couldn't tell if she loved it or hated it. When the tears started to fall, I knew I did something wrong.

"Elisa?"

"I'm sorry," she said as she tried to wipe her tears away. "It's very sweet, Jared."

"Then why are you crying?"

She stood up and turned away from me, the locket forgotten on the bed. "I—I can't do this. I'm sorry."

I felt my heart fall. "What—what do you mean?"

She started to sob. "I thought I was ready but obviously I'm not. I'm sorry. I'm so sorry."

I felt the tears burn behind my eyes but they didn't fall. "Please don't do this, Elisa."

"I'm sorry, Jared. I like you, I really do, but I can't do this."

I looked at the floor and tried to control my breathing. I didn't understand. I did everything for this girl. I knew she would never be over her husband and I was fine with that. "Elisa, don't be scared. It's okay. Just sleep on it tonight."

"No," she said. She still wouldn't look at me. "I can't do this, Jared. I'm sorry. I want you to leave."

"Please don't do this."

"You told me that if I ever asked you to leave, you would do it without hesitation."

She was right. I did say that. I rose from the bed but couldn't feel my legs. I thought everything was fine. We seemed so happy together. The kids loved me. I didn't want this to happen. "Uh—I'll go."

"Okay," she whispered. She didn't bother to turn around.

I came up behind her but didn't touch her. "Elisa, I love you."

She was silent.

I turned and left the room. When I reached the front door, I almost didn't walk through. But I knew there was nothing I could do. I don't know what I did to deserve this but I obviously did something. I opened the door then closed it behind me. When I walked out to the street, I couldn't see where I was going through the tears in my eyes.

Somehow I ended up at my apartment. When I collapsed on the couch, I stared at the wall for a long time, not even thinking. Then the tears burst from my eyes and cascaded down my face. I controlled my breathing after a moment and stifled my cries. Elisa was the love of my life. I couldn't believe this was happening. I went into my bedroom but I didn't sleep. I just lay there.

# 11

I called in sick the next day. I would have loved the distraction but I would see Ethan, who reminded me of Elisa. If I spoke to him, I knew I would break down. I knew my relationship with Elisa was going to be complicated, but after she slept with me, I assumed that we were serious. I told her not to sleep with me unless that's how she felt. She didn't even tell me why.

I couldn't figure it out. I knew it had something to do with her husband. She was making a new family with me, or just replacing the old one with a new figure. In either scenario, she felt guilty about moving on. I understood her pain but I thought we were past this. I really wished she had figured this out sooner before she ripped out my heart and torched it in flames.

The day went by but I didn't move. I went to the bathroom once but I didn't drink or eat. I just fell in and out of sleep over and over again. I knew I had to go to work the next day but I really didn't want to. I just wanted to lie there.

At some point I got up and moved into the living room. I tried to watch television to get my mind off Elisa. Nothing worked. Even when I watched a commercial of an auto repair shop I somehow thought of her. I thought about calling her but I knew I couldn't. She didn't want to talk to me. She wanted nothing to do with me. It was the worst pain of my life. When my parents divorced, I was hurt and confused but it was nothing compared to this. Now I felt like I could die.

The sun set over the horizon and left my apartment dark. I didn't turn on the lights. The only illumination was the glow from the television, which I still wasn't watching.

There was a knock on the door but I ignored it. It was probably a school girl selling Christmas cookies or some bullshit. The knock sounded again but I didn't flinch.

"Please open the door."

I recognized her voice. I was still for a long moment before I rose from the couch. When I reached the door, I looked through the peephole. Elisa was standing on the other side. After a moment of staring, I opened it.

She stared at me with a saddened expression. I wondered how I looked to her—probably dead. I was still wearing the same clothes from the day before. I took off my jacket and tie but the pants and shirt were the same. They were wrinkled and worn. I didn't say anything. I didn't know what to say.

"Hey," she said as she looked at me.

"Why are you here?" I asked. My voice came out harsher than I meant. "Please don't check on me. You're just making this harder for me. I don't want to see you."

"I'm sorry about everything," she blurted. "I take it back."

I stared at her for a moment. "What?"

"I'm sorry." Tears started to bubble in her eyes. "I don't want to lose you, Jared. I was just—emotional last night. I'm so sorry. I want you back. Please don't go."

I took a deep breath. "You mean it?"

She wiped a tear away. "Of course I do."

I grabbed her and squeezed her to my chest. "Thank god." I buried my face in her neck and let my tears leak. I was so happy that she came back to me. I was shaking.

"I'm sorry."

"Just forget about it, Ellie."

She rubbed her fingers through my hair then down my back. "That necklace just scared me, Jared. I'm really moving on. Sometimes I get cold feet. I feel like I'm betraying Tom."

I pulled away and looked at her. "I'm sorry that I rushed you and tried too hard."

"It wasn't you, Jared."

"Since we slept together, I assumed—"

"I know. I'm sorry."

"Next time just ask for your space. Don't break up with me. It almost killed me, Elisa."

"Please don't say that."

"Okay."

"Jared, I'm so sorry."

"You're forgiven." I kissed her forehead then guided her into my apartment. I moved her to the couch and just held her in my arms. We said nothing for a long time. I didn't have anything to say. I was still in shock.

"Come home with me," she whispered.

I looked at her. "You came here by yourself?"

She nodded.

"In the dark?"

"Yeah."

"Why didn't you just call me?"

"I didn't want to do this over the phone."

"You could have asked me to come over."

"I'm sorry."

"Don't do it again." My voice came out cold.

"I'm sorry."

"It's okay," I said. "Let me shower and I'll take you back."

"You'll sleep with me, right?"

"Yeah, of course."

"Okay."

I showered and changed my clothes before we left.

"Does Ethan know?" I asked when we were in the cab.

She nodded.

"What did he say?"

"That I was just getting scared."

"Yeah."

"I'm really sorry for hurting you."

I hate seeing Elisa in pain. She said she was sorry and I believed her. I grabbed her face and directed her gaze on me. "I forgive you, Elisa. Just forget about it. We're okay."

She stared at me for a long time. "Okay."

When we arrived at the house, the kids were sitting in the living room with Ethan and Sadie. Ethan stared at us for a long moment.

Elisa grabbed my hand. "We're going to go to bed early."

Ethan nodded but said nothing.

We walked inside the bedroom and I removed my clothes. Since I hadn't slept all night, I was exhausted. I stripped down to my boxers then lay in bed. Elisa removed her clothes then lay next to me, kissing my chest and neck.

I wasn't in the mood to fool around so I grabbed her and held her to my chest, just holding her tight. The smell of coconut wafted to my nostrils. I felt better having her next to me. I couldn't live without her and I tried to forget about that short amount of time when I was forced to. She hurt me so deeply but I didn't want her to know that. I just wanted to forget about that day. It started off so amazing. I planned to make her birthday perfect but it exploded in my face. When I said I forgave her, I meant it, but remnants of the pain were still there. They would be there for a long time.

# 12

I left early the next morning and went to the gym. I didn't feel like spending the day with Elisa and she didn't ask me to stay. She probably understood that I needed my space. I loved her more than anything and I wanted to be with her but the pain wouldn't stop. My heart was throbbing.

After I finished my boxing class, I went back to my apartment and showered. I spent the Saturday afternoon lounging around the living room. I made lunch and watched television for a while. After I had some time alone, I was feeling better, not so upset. I wondered if I could see Elisa later. A new kid's movie was playing at the theatre. We could take the children then go to ice cream afterwards.

When I reached for my phone, it rang. It was Ethan.

"What's up?" I said.

"Are we meeting at the apartment or the restaurant?"

"What?"

"I called Elisa but she isn't answering. Sadie and I have been out all day looking at reasonably priced venues to get married. I'm assuming you're with her?"

"Uh—no."

"Oh, we'll just meet you there, then."

"And where are we going?"

"Stella's."

"For what?"

"Elisa's birthday party," he said hesitantly. "You have a bad memory. My family is going to be there. Well, my brothers at least."

"Oh." I still had no idea what he was talking about. Elisa hadn't mentioned anything to me about a birthday party. I don't know how she forgot about it. "Okay, cool."

"See you then."

"Bye."

As soon as I hung up, I called Elisa. She didn't answer so I returned the phone to my pocket. It rang a moment later.

"Hello?" I said.

"Hey," she said happily. "How are you?"

"Good. And you?"

"Good."

"So, do you have plans today?" I waited to hear her response.

"Uh, I have plans with my brother. We're going to dinner."

She was a horrible liar. I could hear it in her voice. "Just you and him?" I asked casually.

"Yeah."

"Oh." I couldn't believe she lied to me.

"You can come over afterwards though."

"Uh, yeah. Hey, I gotta go."

"Oh, okay. I'll see you later."

I hung up. I didn't say bye. I tossed the phone on the table and didn't look at it. She was having a birthday party with her family and she didn't want me there—her boyfriend. Why not? Why didn't she want me to meet her brothers? Ethan obviously approved of me. I slept with her every night. The knowledge broke my heart. And to top it off, she lied to me. It would have broken my heart if she told me the truth but this made it a million times worse. I wasn't just hurt—I was pissed. I felt like she stabbed me through the heart. I thought I actually meant something to her. I thought I was the real deal. Obviously I wasn't. Our relationship was over. I loved her and I didn't want anyone else, but I didn't deserve to be treated like that. She lied to me. I was done.

When evening arrived, I walked down to Stella's and looked through the window. I searched for a while until I saw them sitting at a table in the center of the room. Becky and Tommy were sitting next to Elisa and they wore party hats. A stack of presents was at the edge of the table. She wasn't wearing the necklace I got her. The snow fell down around me and landed on the sidewalk. My breath escaped as a heavy fog. I never felt more alone in my life. I couldn't even talk to my sister because she was sitting at that very table. After I couldn't stand to watch a moment longer, I turned and walked back to my apartment. Before I walked into the building, I stopped. Instead, I pulled out my phone and pressed the send button.

"Hey, what are you're doing tonight?" I asked.

"John and I are at McGrath's," Alex said.

"I'll be there in a second."

"What? You're coming?"

"Yeah." I hung up and headed toward the bar a few blocks away. When I arrived, I grabbed a beer from the bar then joined them at the table. "What's going on?"

Alex clapped me on the shoulder. "Wow. I'm surprised to see you."

"Yeah." I took a drink of my beer.

John stared at me. He and I went to college together. "You okay?"

"I'm fine," I said.

Alex wasn't buying it. "Something happened with Elisa?"

"No. We just broke up."

"What? You did?" he asked incredulously.

"Well, not yet. I'll dump her later."

Alex's mouth dropped. "I thought this chick was the love of your life? You were going to marry her?"

"I thought the same thing but shit happens."

"What did she do?"

"I just don't want to be with her anymore."

"Did she cheat on you?" he asked.

I sighed. "First, she dumped after I planned this amazing birthday for her. I took her back in a heartbeat like an idiot. Then she lied to me about a birthday party she was having with her family. I've been dating her for months, taking care of her kids, fucking her every night, but she doesn't want me to meet her family."

Alex said nothing for a moment. "Wow."

"Yeah," John said. "That's fucked up."

"Just a little," I said sarcastically. I finished my beer and desperately needed another.

"Well, it sounds like she was a lot of work anyway," John said. "A widow with two kids who doesn't even work. Sounds like nothing but baggage."

I didn't respond to his comment. "I need another beer." I left for the bartender again. "Hey," I said to him. "Another one of these." I slid the glass to him.

He stared at me for a moment before he refilled it with the tap. While I waited, I noticed the beautiful brunette sitting next to me. I glanced at her legs then quickly looked away.

"Hey," she said as she smiled at me. "Is that beer for me?"

"No," I said quickly. "Get your own."

"Girls like me don't have to get anything."

I laughed then turned to her. "At least you aren't cocky about it."

"Not at all," she said with a smile.

She had brown eyes that matched her locks. She had well-defined breasts and a beautiful skin tone. It was tan but not too dark. I took a drink of my beer while I stared at her. "Well, have a good night." I turned and walked away.

"Aren't you going to ask for my number, or are you just playing hard to get?"

I smiled at her. "Thanks, but no thanks." I turned and walked away but stopped. Elisa wasn't the right girl for me. She ended our relationship when she broke my heart twice. She didn't care about me and I shouldn't care about her. "Actually," I said as I turned around. "I will take that number."

"Was that playing hard to get?"

"Did it work?"

"No," she said as she picked up a pen and scribbled on a napkin. "But you're cute. That's what worked."

I grabbed the napkin and shoved into my pocket. "And what's your name?" I noticed she didn't write it down.

"You'll find out when you call me. It will make it more interesting that way."

"Do you want to know mine?"

"Not really," she said with smile. She turned away and started talking to the girl sitting next to her. I walked back to the table with a smile on my face.

Alex's dropped jaw almost touched the table. "Are you being serious right now?"

"What?" I said as I sat down.

"You just scored a chick? What about Elisa?"

"I didn't sleep with her—calm down."

"But aren't you still with her?"

"She obviously isn't with me," I said bitterly. I took another drink of my beer. I was going to need another one soon. I was drinking it like filtered water.

"Damn," John said. "She fucked you up."

"Yeah. Good for her."

Alex said nothing for a moment. "Well, I'm glad you're back even though you're miserable."

"Thanks," I said with a laugh. "What a sweet thing to say."

"So when are you going to tell her?"

"Whenever she feels like giving me the time of day," I snapped.

Alex shook his head. "She's a bitch. Fuck her."

I glared at him. "You just crossed a line."

He held up his hands. "Sorry."

I dropped my look of hate and looked across the bar.

Alex looked at me. "But she's obviously stupid. You're a catch. She's a widow with two kids. She isn't going to find a better guy to put up with that."

I shook my head. "I'm done talking about it." I finished my glass of beer then stared at it.

"Thirsty?" John asked.

"Parched," I answered.

Alex stared at me, seeing my eyelids droop from the alcohol. I just drank two beers in less than five minutes. "Maybe that's enough for a while."

"Don't worry about me," I snapped.

He fell silent.

I looked around the bar and caught the girl I talked to looking at me. "I'll see you later." I rose from the chair.

"Where are you going?" Alex asked.

"Home."

He rose from the chair. "I'm going to head out too."

I glared at him. "I don't need to be walked home like a pussy." I turned and left the bar.

I walked down the street, passing the cars and the people on the sidewalk. The snow crunched under my feet as I moved. I stuck my hands in my pockets as I walked. The bitter chill was biting my fingers. It stung.

Somehow I ended up at Elisa's house. I meant to go to my apartment but my buzzed mind and muscled legs had other plans. I stared at the house for a long time. Ethan hung Christmas lights around the window and on the tree in the front yard. There was a sign that said, *Santa, come here*. I don't know how long I stood there, but my nose was so cold that I couldn't feel it. I didn't know what I was waiting for. I just stood there.

"Jared?"

I turned and saw them walk up the street. Elisa had a surprised look on her face when she approached me. Ethan had Tommy on his shoulders and he held a few birthday bags in his hands. Sadie had Becky and a few gifts as well. I stared at Elisa and ignored the rest of them.

"Jared?" she repeated. She stopped in front of me with a frightened expression. Her eyes were wide with fear. She should be scared.

"Did you have a wonderful birthday?" I snapped. I knew how pissed I looked even though I couldn't see my expression. "It looks like you did. Look at all these gifts," I said as I looked at Ethan and Sadie. "What a great night with your family—the people that mean something to you. I guess it wasn't just you and Ethan, after all."

She swallowed the lump in her throat as she looked at me. When she tucked a strand of hair behind her ear, I knew she was nervous.

That just pissed me off even more. Before I spoke, I looked at Tommy. He was staring at me with a frightened expression. He had never seen me angry before. I had never been that pissed so I knew I was absolutely terrifying.

I leaned toward Elisa's ear. "Put *your* kids inside," I whispered.

Ethan stared at us but said nothing.

"Go inside," I said with a clenched jaw.

He walked inside the house with Sadie trailing behind him. She flashed me a worried expression before she went through the door.

"Jared, let me explain—"

"Shut the fuck up!"

She stepped back. That was smart.

I closed the gap between us and got in her face. "First, I try to give you the best birthday ever, something I've never done for anyone else. I had your goddamn kids make you birthday presents and I cooked for you. I don't know how to cook, but I did it for you. Then you break my heart and reject my love. Does sleeping with me mean nothing to you?" Spit flew from my mouth as I yelled at her. I was so mad that I could have punched my fist through a vault. "We agreed that if we slept together everything would change—it would be you and me. Were you just lying?"

"No, I—"

"Stop talking," I snapped. "I don't give a shit about your answer. It's just a lie anyway." I glared at her before I continued. Her eyes started to shine with unspent tears. "When you apologized to me, I forgave you because I love you so fucking much, but I shouldn't have done it. You obviously aren't ready for a commitment. You've never been. I told you how I felt about you but you just slept with me because you were horny. You never actually cared for me."

"That isn't true—"

"How many times do I have to tell you to shut up?"

She fell silent.

"Then you go to dinner with your family—your brothers—and purposely keep me away. You obviously don't love me enough to introduce me to them. I thought we were serious, Elisa—a team. I take care of you and your kids, I sleep with you every night, and I love you. But I wasn't good enough to meet your family. You've obviously been using me." I ran my fingers through my hair so I wouldn't punch anything. "And you fucking lied to me— *lied to me*. You obviously have no respect for me. I thought we loved each other—" I paused. Now I knew it wasn't true. "You've never told me that you loved me," I said to myself. I felt stupid. For some reason I thought she said it but she never did. "You've never loved me."

A tear fell from her eyes and she clutched her body tightly, listening to me.

I shook my head. "You've never loved me," I said with a laugh. "God, I'm so stupid." It wasn't funny but I was laughing. I clutched my head for a moment. "Uh. I even introduce you to my dad. You were the first girl I brought home and it was a complete mistake."

She started to cry, tears dripping down her face.

I finally looked at her again. "I'm done with you, Elisa. I love you and would have spent the rest of my life trying to make you happy, helping you live again, but I deserve better than this. You may be better than me, beautiful and amazing, but I'm not putting up with this bullshit."

She wiped her tears away but kept crying. "Jared, please listen to me."

"Have a good life."

"No, please don't go." She grabbed my arm.

I jerked away and glared at her. "I don't want you, Elisa. I'm sick of your bullshit. We could have taken this as slow as you wanted but you wanted to sleep with me—*you*. I would have waited forever. I never want to see you again."

123

She sobbed. "No, please don't go. I'm sorry about everything. I was wrong. Please."

I shook my head then walked past her.

"Jared!"

I ignored her.

"I love you!"

I stopped in my tracks. Anger that I've never felt coursed through my veins in pounding waves. My heart snapped into pieces at her words. I was livid, crazy, and insanely pissed. I turned around and marched up to her. "How dare you say that to me!"

She stepped back.

"That's convenient that you decide to tell me this now. That's so low, Elisa. I hate you." She closed her eyes and averted her gaze. "You don't understand how much I hate you. You didn't just break my heart. You never appreciated anything I did for you. I did everything I possibly could to make you happy. Good luck finding someone to put up with your baggage, your bullshit, your kids, and your lies. Fuck off." I turned and walked away.

She walked behind until she reached me. "Please, Jared. Don't do this. I'm so sorry. I'm so sorry." I kept walking and ignored her. "I mean it. I love you. You're completely right, Jared. My behavior has been unacceptable, but I'll do anything to keep you. I'll change. Please."

When she kept following me, I stopped. "Go home, Elisa."

"Not without you."

I grabbed her by both arms. "Now!"

The tears fell from her eyes. "No."

I didn't want her anymore but I could let her follow me, walk alone on the sidewalk. I didn't want her to be scared in the dark and I didn't want anything to happen to her. I grabbed her arm and marched her to the front door.

"Jared, I love you so much."

"No, you just love my cock and my attention," I snapped.

"It isn't like that."

I came to the front door and opened it. "Go inside," I whispered. My voice was still deadly.

"Not without you."

I tried to push her in but she wouldn't budge.

I picked her up and carried her over the threshold. Ethan was standing in the doorway, staring at me with a worried expression. "Don't let her follow me," I said as I put her down. "It's not my job to protect her anymore."

"Jared! Please don't leave me. I'm sorry about everything."

"I hope you treat the next one better." I glared at her before I left and slammed the door behind me.

# 13

"If you're calling me to discuss Elisa, then just hang up," I snapped. "And if you say her name, I'll hang up."

Sadie said nothing for a moment. "Uh—how are you?"

"Fine," I snapped.

"You wanna get something to eat?"

"I have a date."

"What?"

"I said I have a date."

"With who?"

"A girl."

"Isn't it a little early to be dating?"

"Wasn't it a little early for her to lie to me?"

"Since you mentioned her, can I talk about her now?"

"No," I snapped.

She sighed. "Jared, please give her a chance."

I hung up.

She called me back.

"What?"

"Don't hang up on me."

"Don't talk about her."

"When can I talk about her?"

"I never want to discuss her again."

She sighed.

"You're my fucking sister. You are supposed to be on my side."

"I am."

"It doesn't sound like it."

"Well, I am. I think Elisa was wrong, but I also understand it."

"That's like saying Ethan cheated on you, and even though it was wrong, I understand it."

"Not the same thing at all. Elisa didn't cheat on you."

"She still betrayed me."

"And she was wrong for that."

"But?"

"She's just scared, Jared."

"No! She's just never seen me as a serious boyfriend. I was just there to sleep with her and make her feel better about herself."

"So it's really over?"

"That wasn't clear? Don't you want me to be with someone who actually loves me?"

"Of course I do."

"Then you should hate her as much as I do."

"You don't hate her."

"Yes, I fucking do."

"You're a horrible liar."

"So is she."

"Jared, you really loved this girl."

"And she didn't love me."

"I think she does."

"Do you want me to hang up again?"

"No."

"Then knock it off."

"I want to see you."

"No."

"You can't hide forever."

"Leave me alone, Sadie."

"Does Dad know?"

I was quiet for a moment. "No. Can you tell him for me?"

"Are you sure you want me to? Maybe I should wait."

"No, don't wait. She and I are done."

"Okay," she said quietly.

I heard a knock on the door. "I have to go."

"Okay."

"Bye."

"Jared?"

"What?"

"I love you and I'm on your side."

I took a deep breath. "I love you too."

"Bye."

I hung and returned the phone to my pocket.

I went to the door and answered it. I had a date with Layla, the girl I met at the bar, but I was supposed to meet at her place. She didn't even know where I lived.

When I saw Elisa on the other side of the door, I felt the anger return. I didn't want to see her. We hadn't spoken in a week. I would let myself think about her. "What?"

She tucked her hair behind her ear. She looked beautiful like usual. She wore a black cardigan that clung to her body. The necklace I got her hung around her neck. "Can we talk for a second?" Her voice was weak.

"There's nothing to talk about. Now go away."

"Please," she begged. "Just give me a minute."

"It won't change anything."

"Please." She stared at me with wide eyes.

"Hurry. I'm on my way out."

"Can I come in?"

I ignored her question.

"You're right. I didn't treat you right and I regret it. I didn't invite you to my birthday dinner because I was scared about how serious we had become. I lied to you because I didn't want to hurt your feelings. When I broke up with you, I was just scared—I love you so much and it makes me feel guilty."

I said nothing for a moment. "Or you were never serious about me and you always wanted to keep me as your dirty little secret."

"Not at all, Jared."

"If you weren't ready then why did you act like you were?? I would have understood all of that if we hadn't moved forward. You made me believe that you loved me when you didn't. I thought we were serious together. You've never been serious about me. You've never wanted me."

"Jared, I love you so much. I slept with you because I loved you. You're right. We shouldn't have done that since I haven't overcome the guilt I feel, but I want to be with you. I don't want this to end."

"You lied to me."

"I was going to tell you the truth when I saw you."

"I'm sure," I said sarcastically.

"It's true."

"Coming from the queen of liars."

She started to cry and wiped her tears away. I watched for a moment without any pity. When I saw her alone in the hallway, I got angry again.

"You came here by yourself? What the hell were you thinking?" I grabbed my jacket then walked out the door. "I'll take you home but don't come back here. I mean it." When I turned down the hall, I saw Ethan leaning against the wall.

"She asked me to bring her here," he said.

I said nothing for a moment. "Well, that makes up for everything," I said sarcastically.

Ethan ran his fingers through his hair as he looked me. "Elisa was wrong for what she did. I admit it and she admits it. But please give her another chance. You love her and she loves you."

I laughed. "Wow. Talk about a 180."

He didn't laugh or smile. "Jared, please give her another chance. The situation is complicated and you know it."

Elisa looked at me. "I was wrong and I've changed. It won't happen again. I'm ready to commit to you in every way. I—I just made a mistake. I love you, Jared."

I didn't look at her. "No."

Ethan sighed. "Don't do this. I know you love her."

"That wasn't enough then and it isn't enough now."

Elisa grabbed my arm. "Please, Jared. I don't want you to leave."

"I'm already gone," I whispered. I pulled my arm away. "Excuse me. I have a date."

Elisa dropped her arm then covered her face. She started to sob as she stepped away. "A—date?"

I didn't say anything.

She sobbed quietly to herself.

"Goodbye," I said. "Don't bother me ever again."

Ethan grabbed me. "Don't do this."

I pushed him back. "You were always riding my ass about hurting your sister but I treated her with nothing but respect and love. I put her on a pedestal and treated her like a fucking goddess, and you have the goddamn nerve to expect me to put up with her bullshit? What about me? She ripped my heart out of my chest, broke up with me, lied to me, and you expect me to just let that go?" He said nothing. "If the situations were reversed, you would beat the shit out of me. And you definitely wouldn't let her give me another chance. So as your brother-in-law, give me that same respect." I turned away then walked down the hallway. I took the stairs two at a time until I reached the street. I pushed the thought of Elisa to the back of my mind. She and I were done. I wasn't going to waste my time thinking about her.

When I arrived at Layla's apartment, I plastered a smile on my face and pretended everything was fine.

"You look great," I said as she opened the door. She was wearing a tight fitting dress that fit her body perfectly.

"Thanks. You do too."

"Are you ready?"

"Yes."

We left then walked down the sidewalk. She was wearing a jacket that reached her knees but she still looked cold. I took off my jacket and wrapped it around her shoulders. She smiled at me as we walked. I didn't put my arm around her or touch her.

When we arrived at the restaurant, we sat by the window. She looked beautiful as she stared at me. I could tell she was seriously interested in me by the way she was looking at me.

"Have you finished all your Christmas shopping?" she asked.

"Yeah. Have you?"

"I always do mine on black Friday."

I shivered. "That sounds horrible. People actually die doing that."

She laughed. "I always bring my bullet proof vest and my gun."

I laughed. "At least you take it seriously."

"Yeah."

"So, where do you work?"

"I'm a bartender."

"Oooh. I like bars. You'll have to make me a drink."

"I could make you something special."

"I look forward to it. As long as you don't get me drunk."

"I can't promise anything," she said with a wink. "So what do you do?"

"I work on Wall Street."

"Wow." I heard her ovaries pop. "That's impressive."

I shrugged. "It's alright."

"So you must be smart."

"You would think."

"You're humble. I like it."

I didn't say anything.

"I'm surprised a catch like you is single."

I immediately thought of Elisa but then I pushed the thought to the back of my mind. "Not everyone thinks I'm a catch."

"I seriously doubt that."

I said nothing.

She reached across the table and ran her fingers over my knuckles. "So tell me something."

"What do you want to know?"

"Did you just want to sleep with me, or did you want something more with me?"

"I don't think I know you well enough to choose."

"Well, I'm down for either one."

I felt my skin prickle.

"Does that help you choose?"

I cleared my throat. "Same question."

She smiled. "I would like something more."

"But you don't know me."

"I know enough." She continued to stroke my hand.

When the waiter came to our table, I was relieved. We ordered before he walked away and it was only a few minutes later when he returned with our glasses of wine.

She took a big drink from it. "You have good taste."

"Thank you."

"Maybe we should take a bottle back to my place."

"Sure." I leaned back in my chair then looked out the window.

"What are you thinking about?"

"How long your legs are."

"I can show you."

"Are you always this forward?"

"No. I just really like you."

"You're lucky I'm such a gentleman."

"Or unlucky."

I smiled. I liked her wit.

"So have you ever been married?"

"No. Have you?"

"No."

"Then why do you ask?"

"I thought you might be divorced since you're single."

"No."

"Have any kids?"

"No. Do you?"

"No."

I drank from my wine while I stared at her.

"What do you like for breakfast?"

I raised an eyebrow.

"Just answer the question."

"Uh—pancakes, bacon, and eggs."

"I'll make it tomorrow."

I almost spit out my wine. I somehow managed to get it down. Her smile widened as she looked at me.

"You interested?"

"Uh, yeah."

"Good."

The waiter brought our food and we started to eat. Our conversation turned to television shows and music. Her favorite movie was the Godfather, which surprised me. I wondered what Elisa's favorite movie was. She told me that she used to play the guitar and she was quite good. That was impressive. It turned out that we went to the same gym even though I had never seen her there before. She was cute, funny, outgoing, and cool. I couldn't find a single flaw in her.

When the waiter brought the check, she looked at him. "Do you want dessert?"

"Of course," he said. "What did you have in mind?"

"Something that won't melt."

I understood her meaning.

"We have a chocolate cake," the waiter said.

"We'll take it." She looked at me. "To go. Oh—and a bottle of wine."

"Of course, miss." He turned and walked away.

She looked at me. "I hope that's okay."

"That's more than okay."

"Good."

I felt my heart race in my chest while I looked at her. I knew what she wanted to do with that cake and wine. It was going to be messy. I felt my sweat under my shirt. It suddenly got very hot. When the waiter returned with the bill, I handed him the cash and grabbed the to-go box and the bottle of wine.

We made it out to the street and walked down the sidewalk. She moved close to me and wrapped her arm around my waist. My heart rate increased. I was strangely aware of my body and the feel of her touch. We continued to walk but I didn't pay attention to where we were going. I was too nervous.

When we arrived at her apartment, she opened her clutch and searched for her keys. I swallowed the lump in my throat while I waited. I was really going through with this. She finally got the door opened and we walked inside.

She grabbed the wine and cake from my hand, set it on the counter, then she turned to me.

"I would hate to get that suit dirty," she said as she placed her hands on my chest and pushed the jacket from my shoulders. I let it fall.

I placed my hands on her waist and felt the smooth material of the dress. I could feel her curves easily.

She pressed her face close to mine. I could smell the alcohol on her breath. It was sweet and strong. Layla grabbed my tie then yanked on it, pulled my lips to hers. Her kiss was soft and warm. She parted my lips with her tongue and slipped it inside. I tasted the wine.

Elisa's face popped into my mind. I remembered how I felt when I kissed her. Every time I touched her lips, I felt like I would explode. Flashes of our lovemaking blinded me. I couldn't even feel Layla's lips anymore. All I thought about was Elisa. I remembered the day we spent at the park, every morning when we had breakfast together, the way she would kiss me when I came over. It wouldn't stop. I remembered how horrible I felt when she dumped me, breaking my heart. The night when she lied to me burned the inside of my skull. I was in pain but I couldn't stop thinking about her. I couldn't forget her.

"I can't do this." I pulled away.

She stared at me for a moment, her mouth still opened.

"I'm sorry," I said as I averted my gaze.

She grabbed my face and kissed me again. "Come on. I want you, Jared."

I kissed her again but Elisa returned. "No."

"Why?"

"I—I'm in love with someone else."

I expected her to get mad, throw the bottle of wine at my head, but she didn't. "I'm okay with that."

"What?"

"Well, why aren't you with this girl?"

"Because I can't."

"Then you need to move on."

"I know."

"Let me help you." She started to kiss my neck. "I'll make you forget her."

I moaned and gave into the feeling for a moment. I wanted to forget about Elisa and I knew sleeping with someone else would be the first step but I couldn't do it. "I'm sorry. You're great. I—I'm just not ready." I pulled away.

She sighed in frustration. "Fine. I'll wait."

I said nothing.

She kept her hands on my chest.

"I should go. I'm sorry about this."

"It's okay," she said as she ran her fingers through my hair.

"It's nothing personal."

"I know," she said. "I'll save the wine for another time."

I didn't say anything. I pulled away and walked toward the door.

"She's a very lucky lady."

I stopped before I walked out the door. "Tell her that."

# 14

Instead of going home right away, I went to a bar. It was crowded but I didn't notice anyone. I was in my own world. I hated what I was feeling. I couldn't be with Elisa but I couldn't move on from her either. We had been broken up for only a week but I wanted to move on already. I just didn't want to feel this pain anymore.

I opened my wallet and looked at the picture of Tommy and Becky. I put a copy in my wallet when I got Elisa that necklace. I missed them. They weren't my kids but I loved them like my own. I wondered if they asked about me. I wondered if they missed me.

The morning when I made the paintings with the kids was a moment I'll never forget. It was the first time I was completely alone with them. I loved every second of it. They were messy, loud, and hyper, but they were adorable at the same time. They were nothing but work, but it was the kind of work that left you satisfied at the end of the day. When I thought about never seeing them again, it made me want to cry.

When I finally walked home it was late. There weren't as many people on the sidewalk. The snow was falling but I didn't feel cold. Perhaps it was the alcohol. Perhaps it was because I was too numb to feel anything. It didn't matter which.

I got inside the elevator and leaned against the wall. I watched the lights change as the elevator ascended the floors. When the light shined over the third floor, I thought of Sadie. When she lived in the same building, she was always a short distance away. Now she was across town—with Elisa. I missed her and Koku. I felt like I lost my best friend. I felt uncomfortable talking to her about Elisa. Since she was Ethan's sister, it was awkward. When I vented about Suzie, it was never an issue.

When the doors finally opened, I stumbled out. I stared at the floor as I walked to my apartment. When I reached the entrance, I dropped my keys. Elisa was sitting in front of my door.

I stared at her in surprise. I didn't expect her to be there.

"Hey," she said with a quivering lip. Her eyes immediately appeared soaked.

I cleared my throat. "Why are you here?"

"I'm not giving up on you," she whispered.

"I've already moved on."

She was quiet for a moment. "Have you slept with her?"

"It's none of your business whether I did or not."

She nodded but continued to cry.

"Please leave me alone, Elisa."

"Ellie," she corrected.

I said nothing.

She didn't move from her seat in front of my door. "I'm not leaving, Jared. Not until you talk to me."

I looked at my watch. "It's one in the morning."

"I planned to wait all night if I had to."

I glared at her. "Did you walk here in the middle of the night by yourself?" My tone sounded like I unleashed a death threat. My eyes were wide with anger.

She said nothing.

"Your answer better be no."

She still didn't say anything.

I kneeled down in front of her. "If I wasn't a gentleman, I would slap you so fucking hard."

A tear fell down her cheek as she looked at me.

"I don't want you walking around by yourself—especially at night."

"Why do you care?"

"What? Of course I care."

"Why?"

"How could you do that to me? If you love me, you wouldn't risk your life like this. The streets are dangerous in the day and the night, but especially past ten. What the fuck were you thinking?"

"I had to see you."

"What's the point if you have to risk your life?"

"I had to."

"Elisa, you have kids to think about."

"I know," she whispered.

"Why do you keep hurting me?" I snapped. "I would die if something happened to you."

She wiped her tears away. "You won't answer my calls and you wouldn't come to me if I asked you to."

"You could ask Ethan."

"He wouldn't bring me."

I stared at her. "Then you shouldn't have come."

"I love you. I want you to know that I do."

I remained silent.

"And I know your answer is no."

I raised an eyebrow. "What?"

"You didn't sleep with her."

She was right but I would never tell her that.

"You love me and don't want anyone else. Jared, give me another chance. I won't let you down. I don't just want you now but for my whole life."

I rose to a stand and took a deep breath. "Let's get out of the hall."

She climbed to her feet and looked at me.

I put my key in the door then unlocked it. We walked inside and I threw my key on the counter then dropped my jacket on a chair. When I looked at her, more tears started to fall from her eyes. I ignored her and walked into my room, removing my tie and unbuttoning my shirt. When I looked at my collar, I saw the lipstick stain. Now I knew why she was crying. I sighed. I didn't know that was there.

After I changed, I went back into the living room and she was crying on the couch. I sat beside her and rested my hands on my knees.

"I didn't sleep with her," I said.

She continued to cry.

"I kissed her—that's it."

She sniffed.

"I thought I was ready to move on but I'm not."

She finally looked at me. "Please give me another chance. Please. I never meant to hurt you. I promise that I'm ready now. I want a life with you, Jared. I'm sorry that I was so stupid before."

I wanted to be with her so much. I loved her and I wanted this to work, but I knew she would never be ready for a real relationship. I trusted her once and I couldn't do it again. She already broke my heart twice. I didn't want her to damage me beyond repair. I still had a chance to find happiness in someone else. If I let her hurt me over and over, then I would never be able to trust anyone. "Elisa, let me make this clear. We are over—done."

She looked away and clutched her stomach.

"I'm not saying this to hurt you. I can't trust you, Elisa. You say that you're ready to move on but you clearly aren't. And there's nothing wrong with that. I don't know what it's like to lose a spouse. I couldn't even imagine. So it's okay not to be ready."

"I am ready, Jared. I'm sorry that I had to lose you to realize it."

"I wish I could believe you," I whispered.

She grabbed my hand. "You can. Please."

I closed my eyes. "No. Stop making this so hard for me."

She wrapped her arms around my neck and held me close. "I can't lose you. I can't."

I kissed her forehead. "Elisa, if you ever need anything, I'm always there for you. It doesn't matter if it's next week or next year. I'll always help you. Even if I'm married and have kids of my own."

She sobbed at my words.

"But I can't do this. I can't be in a relationship unless you're in it too."

"I am in it."

"For two months you weren't there, Elisa. A part of you was, but not as much as there should have been. I said I would settle for a piece of your heart but you didn't give my any of it."

"It's yours now."

"It's too late, Elisa."

She pressed her forehead against mine. "The kids miss you so much."

I sighed. "Please don't do this to me."

"Then be with me."

"I deserve better."

"I'll give you everything you need."

"I wish I could believe you."

"Don't try to move on with someone else if I'm the woman you really love. Try to work this out with me."

"I have to try."

"No."

"I'm sorry." I pulled her hands from my neck then stood up. "I'll take you home now."

"Sleep with me."

"I can't do that."

"Please."

"No."

"I can't sleep without you, Jared. Please give me one night. Please."

"I know what you're trying to do."

"My request is genuine."

"I'll let you sleep in my room and I'll sleep on the couch—that's it."

"No. It has to be you."

"I can't do that."

"Please."

"Stop torturing me!"

She stiffened at my words.

"Now I'm taking you home. Let's go."

She rose to her feet but averted her gaze. I grabbed my jacket then opened the door for her.

"You don't need to walk me home, Jared."

"Don't be stupid," I snapped. "I want to walk you home."

She stared at me for a moment before she stepped through. I locked the door behind us and we left the building. She didn't speak to me and I didn't say anything to her. She rubbed her arms as we walked down the sidewalk. I took off my jacket and covered her with it, keeping her warm. She smiled at me but it was a weak one.

When we walked by a group of thugs leaning against the wall, she moved closer to me, frightened. I wrapped my arm around her and held her close to me. "Don't be scared," I whispered.

We walked to the townhouse and climbed the stairs. I waited for her to find her keys in her purse. She took a long time to pull them out, and when she did have them, she just held them in her hand.

"Good night," I whispered.

"No."

"I'm sorry."

She looked at me with her sad eyes. The tears were forming again.

"I hate seeing you in pain."

"I hate seeing *you* in pain."

I averted my gaze. "Please go inside."

"Come with me."

I hadn't been able to sleep without her either. And when I did sleep, all I dreamt about was her. When I spent the night with Elisa, I had a dreamless slumber and always felt rested. I took a deep breath. "Okay."

She smiled. "Really?"

I nodded.

She unlocked the door and we crept inside. We moved down the hallway and entered her bedroom. She started to remove her clothes but I steadied her. "No."

I pulled down the covers and lay down. I was still fully dressed in my shirt and jeans. I didn't want this night to lead to other things. It would just make it harder. She climbed in beside me and wrapped her arms around me, resting her head on my chest. I indulged in my desires and held her tightly, smelling the scent of her hair. Her skin was smooth and soft. She was so small in my arms. I grabbed my phone from my pocket and set my alarm for early in the morning, before anyone else would wake up. I placed it on the nightstand.

"Good night," she whispered to me.

"Good night."

She raised her head and looked at me. "I love you, Jared."

I swallowed the lump in my throat. "I love you, Ellie."

# 15

"Mom!"

The light from the window lingered behind my eyelids. I vaguely felt aware of Elisa's small form in my arms. Her hair was scattered across my skin. I felt rested and refreshed even though I was still asleep.

"Mommy, make us breakfast! Uncle Ethan won't make French toast."

I sat up in bed, knocking Elisa to the side. What time was it? When I looked at the clock, it was ten in the morning. My alarm was set for six. I grabbed my phone and looked at it. It didn't go off and I set the time right. I wasn't sure what happened.

Elisa sighed. "I'll be there in a second." She stretched on the bed then reached for me, wrapping her arms around me.

"My alarm didn't go off," I said in a frantic voice.

"What happened?"

"I don't know. I'm sorry."

"It's okay. The kids will be happy to see you."

I looked at her, suspicion clouding my mind. "You turned off my alarm?"

She grabbed my face and kissed me. I immediately melted at the touch of her lips. I hadn't kissed her in so long. She ran her fingers through my hair and pulled me toward her. Paralyzed by her embrace, I let her climb on top of me and kiss me harder. Against my restraint, I let my

146

hands run through her hair and cup her face. Her cheek was so soft. I loved every inch of her. She was gorgeous.

Elisa pulled off her shirt and I felt my heart accelerate. Her breasts popped out of her bra and looked round and firm. I knew I needed to stop this. She was seducing me and I had to end it. When she kissed me again, I became weak, giving into my desires for her. I never felt more attracted to a woman than I was to her. She was breathtaking. While we kissed, she pulled off her pants then her underwear.

"Stop," I said.

She grabbed my hand and placed my fingers over her cunt. "I'm wet for you."

I moaned. "Damn. Stop."

"No."

I slipped my fingers inside her and watched her mouth open in a moan. "Jared."

"Mommy!" Becky wailed again.

We both ignored her.

Elisa reached her hand in my pants and started to rub me. "Make love to me."

I wanted to stop but I couldn't. "Ellie."

"Tell me you love me."

"I love you like crazy."

She unbuttoned my pants and pulled them off. I didn't stop her. I wanted her too much at that point. I was too far gone. She removed my shirt and I let her. She straddled my hips then inserted me inside of her.

"Fuck," I whispered. She was so damn wet.

She moved on top of me, pressing her forehead against mine. "I love you so much."

"I love you, Ellie."

Elisa had successfully seduced me but I didn't care.

She rocked my hips repeatedly, taking me completely inside her. With every thrust, I felt myself crumble more and more. She felt so good, so amazing. Her lips were on mine in a fiery embrace. I ran my hands through her hair as I made love to her. It always felt right with her. I felt myself about to come but I didn't want to. I wanted to last as long as possible, enjoy this moment.

Her lips stopped moving and she just breathed into my mouth. "Oh yeah."

I thrust into her harder. "Come for me."

"I am," she said as she bit her lip.

I pressed my lips against her ear. "I love you."

"I'm yours, Jared. Completely."

I moaned.

A small yell escaped her lips as she finished her moment. I didn't hear Becky again so I assumed she abandoned her request for breakfast. I thrust into her harder and felt the orgasm start. It burst from my balls and ignited.

"Ellie."

"Yeah."

"Ellie."

"Come on. I want all of you."

I continued to come. "I'm giving it to you."

"Yeah."

When I was done, I pressed my forehead against hers, catching my breath. She looked into my eyes while she breathed heavily. Then she kissed my forehead and rubbed her nose against mine. The intimate touch made me melt.

When Becky banged on the door again, Elisa sighed then climbed off me. I moaned at the loss of her warmth.

"I'm coming, honey."

I covered my face as I realized what just happened. Now I made things more complicated. I couldn't be in this relationship and I just made the break up even harder for both of us. I knew what Elisa was trying to do. If we slept together, made love, then spent time with her kids, I would give in because I couldn't live without her. It was a brilliant plan.

I rolled out of bed then dressed myself. I hoped Ethan and Sadie weren't home. I didn't want to explain myself to them. I wasn't sure what the kids would think when they saw me. They would probably be confused.

Elisa opened the door and Becky came into the room. When she saw me, her eyes lit up like fireworks on the fourth of July and she squealed.

"Uncle Jared!" she dashed to me then wrapped her arms around my legs. "I missed you."

I closed my eyes and felt the tears bubble. I kneeled down and wrapped her in my arms, hiding my face from her view. I held her for a long moment and fought against the tears. I missed her and Tommy so much. I never thought about having kids, and now I had two of them. She felt so small in my arms.

Elisa watched us with a smile on her lips.

I regained my composure then pulled away. "How are you, beautiful?"

"Good! I made more paintings. Mommy let me put them everywhere."

I nodded. "That's where they belong."

Tommy came into the room. He stopped when he saw me. A smile stretched across his face but he said nothing. He ran to me as fast as he could. He almost fell forward but I caught him in my arms. "Where have you been?" he cried. "I couldn't find you."

My eyes started to moisten again. Damn. "I've—just been busy, man."

"Cars aren't fun without you."

I didn't say anything. I didn't know what to say. My life was empty and meaningless without these kids. I finally pulled away and stood up.

"I want breakfast!" Becky said.

Elisa smiled at them. "Alright, alright. I heard you."

"Then why didn't you come?" she asked.

Her cheeks blushed. "I was busy."

Becky and Tommy walked down the hallway and went into the kitchen. Elisa and I followed right behind them. I followed the same routine that I did before we broke up. I sat in my usual seat at the table. The children spoke to me while Elisa cooked.

When Ethan and Sadie walked into the room, they both flinched. I felt my heart fall. I didn't want to be seen. Sadie and Ethan sat down and looked at me but didn't comment, which I was grateful for. I assumed their silence had something to do with the kids.

Elisa served breakfast and we ate in silence. Normally we were talkative during the meal but it was awkward that morning. Ethan and Sadie were curious what my presence meant to the relationship. Elisa smiled at me from across the table, acting like everything was fine. I sincerely hoped she didn't assume that we were back together. She tricked me, disabled my alarm, then seduced me. I'm not blaming her—I should have been stronger—but she still brought this on. Her last defense was the kids. She knew how much I loved them. Perhaps if I was still willing to leave her, I might stay for the kids. I had to harden my heart and not think about that. I still couldn't forget what Elisa did to me. I wasn't one to hold grudges, but I couldn't stand the idea of getting hurt again. Perhaps sleeping together didn't mean anything to her, but that was a promise to me—a sign of her love and commitment to me. She had lied to me and broke my heart. I couldn't do that again.

When breakfast was finished, Elisa cleared the table and washed the dishes in the sink. Like usual, I helped the kids from their booster seats and led them to the living room where their box of toys were. Ethan and Sadie sat on the couch and stared at me. I avoided their look. When I couldn't stand the stares any longer, I went into the kitchen.

When I approached Elisa, I opened my mouth to speak but she kissed me instead, silencing me. I relished her embrace for a moment before I pulled away.

"I should go," I whispered.

"No."

My eyes softened. "Elisa, I'm just going to say everything that I already said."

She closed her eyes for a moment. "You belong here with us. Please don't go. Last night and today meant nothing to you?"

"Of course," I said quickly. "But I didn't want any of that to happen. You're the one that disabled my alarm and climbed on top of me. I wanted to avoid all of that."

She looked away. "I should have stopped it but I was too weak."

"Well, keep being weak."

"I can't."

"Why?"

"I can't trust you, Elisa. I said that already. You aren't ready for a relationship, and I'm too hurt to be patient with you."

"I am ready. I'll marry you today if that's what it takes to convince you."

I sighed. "That isn't how I would want it to go."

"Jared, please don't do this."

"I hate hurting you and I'm sorry for that, but— we're over."

She looked away from me then stared at the dishes in the sink. I said nothing for a long time while she composed herself. The kids and her brother were in the next room. I knew she wanted to hide behind a mask. "Then go," she said. She didn't look at me.

"Are you going to walk me out?"

"No," she whispered. "I'm not going to watch you leave my life forever. I can't do it."

I felt the tears under my eyes but I blinked them back. I hated hearing the despair in her voice. It was worse than hearing her cry. I came up behind her and kissed her on the back of the neck. "I'll always love you, Ellie." I stepped away then walked through the living room without looking at anyone. I didn't say goodbye to the kids. I couldn't. It was too hard.

When I closed the door behind me, I broke down again. The tears fell down my face in waves. I shouldn't have stayed overnight. I shouldn't have made this more painful for the both of us.

# 16

After a few days, I realized the pain was never going to go away. I would always suffer without her. I wanted to turn to Sadie but I couldn't. Now I felt like she was more of a family member to Ethan and Elisa than she was to me. Everything reminded me of Elisa and I hated it. I couldn't do this anymore. I picked up my phone and pressed the send button.

My mom was enthused like she always was. "Hello, darling! How are you? I haven't spoken to you in a month."

"I'm good. You?"

She immediately noticed my despair. "What's wrong, baby?"

"I'm just getting over a cold."

"Oh. I thought you sounded different."

"Yeah."

"So what's new with you?"

"Nothing. There's actually a reason why I called."

"And what is that?"

"Do you know of any job openings in London?"

"What kind of job openings?" she asked hesitantly.

"Business related."

She couldn't contain her excitement. "Does my baby want to move to London?"

"I'm thinking about it."

"I'll ask Roger when I see him. He works for a magazine. And if not, I'll check at work. With your credentials, I'm sure we can find you something."

"Sounds great."

"I'll give you a ring when I found out."

I sighed. "Mom, you aren't even British."

"I live here, don't I?"

I rolled my eyes. "I'll talk to you later."

"Bye, baby. I love you."

"I love you too."

We hung up.

I didn't want to do this but I didn't see any alternative.

My phone rang again and I grabbed it, hoping it was my mother. It was Layla.

"Hey."

"Wow. What's wrong?"

"What do you mean?"

"You sound dead."

I sighed. "I've been better."

"Do you want to talk about it?"

I usually told Sadie everything, and if not her, then Alex or my dad. I couldn't talk to any of them about this. "Actually, yes."

"How about some coffee? We'll have girl talk."

"This isn't gossip hour."

"But it is."

I laughed. "Fifteen minutes?"

"Yep. I'll see you at Queen's Coffee."

"Okay."

I hung up then grabbed my jacket before I walked out the door. When I arrived at the café, she was already sitting in the corner. I didn't order anything to drink because I wasn't thirsty. I hadn't been craving anything in a while. The past three days blended together like a single blur. I had never been more depressed in my life.

"So, what's up?" she asked.

"I'm moving to London."

"What?"

"Yeah."

"That's random."

"Not really."

"Job offer?"

"More like job seeking."

"Don't you work on Wall Street? Did something happen?"

"My job is fine. That's not why I'm leaving."

"It's because of that girl?"

I nodded.

"And why are you moving to another country to get away from her? There are plenty of places *within* the country you can choose from."

I sighed. "Nothing will remind me of her there. We'll be in different time zones. I'll never see her or anyone that reminds me of her."

"What about your family? Your friends?"

"I can't be around them either. My sister is my best friend but she's engaged to this girl's brother. I feel like I'm not even related to her anymore. I can't talk to her about anything. It's a conflict of interest. And I can't tell her anything because she'll tell Elisa."

"Elisa?"

"That's her name. I just need to leave. I'm never going to move on unless I do."

"How long? Forever?"

"A year—maybe two."

"Well, you might meet someone there and never move back. That's always a possibility."

"I really doubt that."

She was quiet for a moment. "When are you going to leave?"

"As soon as my mom finds me a job."

"Does she live there?"

"Yeah. I'll probably stay there for a while."

"Are you going to tell Elisa or your sister?"

"No. They'll just try to stop me. I want to be around my sister again but I can't do that with the way I feel. I want to get over Elisa before I move back. I don't want to make everything awkward. I want everything to be okay."

"And the only way you can do that is in another country?"

"Yeah."

"Damn. You got it bad."

"You have no idea."

"She's so lucky."

I didn't say anything.

"Well, I have family in London."

"Really?"

"Yep. My dad is British."

"What are the odds?"

She shrugged. "I can come with you and show you around for a few days. You probably need help moving anyway."

"You would do that?" I asked incredulously.

"Yeah. I have some time off. And we're friends, right? Since you confided in me, you must not have anyone else."

I laughed. "It's not that. I can't tell anyone close to me because they'll tell someone else and it will get back to Elisa. I'm afraid if she tries to stop me, she'll succeed."

"That makes sense."

"Layla, I have to make this clear." She stared at me. "If you're doing this just as a friend, that's great, but if you're hoping for something more, you're wasting your time. I'm not emotionally or physically available right now. I don't want to hurt you."

She smiled. "Thank you for your honesty. I do want something to happen with you and I'm willing to wait until you're ready."

"Please don't wait. I don't know when I'll ever be ready to move on."

"Sleep with me."

"What?"

"Let's go back to my apartment and get it over with."

"That's romantic."

She laughed. "Rip off the bandage, Jared."

"Do you really want me to sleep with you if I'm thinking of someone else the whole time?"

"No matter how long you wait, you're going to think of Elisa during your first time. It doesn't matter when it is or who it's with. And I'm okay with that. It will help you move forward. Trust me."

I said nothing for a long time. "No—I can't do that."

"Just try."

"No. I slept with Elisa a few days ago. I can't sleep with someone else so soon. That's just—unacceptable."

"You slept with her?"

I nodded. "She climbed on top of me and I was too weak to stop it."

"You're not doing anything wrong, Jared."

"Please drop it," I whispered.

She leaned back in her chair and looked at me.

"You're gorgeous, Layla. That's obvious. And you're awesome. You're funny, sweet, caring, easygoing, kinky, everything I would want in a girl. If things were different, I would probably be in love with you already, but that's not reality. The truth is, I love someone else even though I wish I didn't. Please don't take it personally. The only reason I'm not taking advantage of you is because I'm heartbroken and crippled."

"I know, Jared. It's okay. You don't need to explain."

I nodded.

"But I still want to go with you to London."

"Really?"

"Yeah. It will be fun."

"Thanks. I appreciate it."

My phone rang in my pocket. When I looked at the screen, I saw my mother's name.

"Hey," I said.

"I have wonderful news, baby."

"What is it?"

"Roger has an opening for a business executive for the office. Are you interested?"

"The hours and the pay?"

Weekends off, and you're off at four. It pays forty five thousand pounds."

"No. That's not enough."

"In the states, that's roughly ninety thousand."

"Oh," I said. "Then I'll take it."

"Yay! That's wonderful. When can you get here?"

"Well, I need to put my two weeks in and move."

"You can't wait two weeks. I was thinking a few days at the most."

"You're right. I'll figure it out. When is the interview?"

"Roger said that's unnecessary with your credentials and experience. My baby went to Harvard."

I rolled my eyes even though she couldn't see me.

"So, you're sure about this?"

I was quiet for a moment. I didn't see any alternative. I needed to get over Elisa and I couldn't do that when we lived in the same city. "Yeah."

"I'm so happy! Let me know when you're leaving. And you're staying with me, of course."

"Thanks, Mom."

"Goodbye, honey. Love you."

"Love you too."

She hung up then I returned the phone to my pocket.

"Well, it's official."

"You're really doing this?"

"Yep."

"When?"

"As soon as possible."

"Well, let's get packing."

I felt my heart accelerate. "I guess."

Layla and I grabbed a pizza and went back to the apartment. We started to pack everything while we drank bottles of beer and ate pizza directly from the box. She was almost like one of the boys. It was a shame that I was in love with Elisa. Layla was someone I could really like. Although if Elisa hadn't broken my heart, then I wouldn't have met Layla to begin with. The whole situation sucked. Of all the women in Manhattan, why did I have to fall in love with a widow with two children who still wasn't able to move on? I have the worst taste in women—seriously. Suzie was just a psychopath and Elisa was a heartbreaker. I had serious issues.

Since I wasn't taking any of my furniture overseas, I just packed my belongings. I didn't have a lot of things to take with me. Just my clothes and accessories. I would sell all the extra stuff to the landlord so he could rent out the apartment as already furbished. It was just easier that way.

When we were done, Layla and I watched television on the couch. She snuggled up next to me but I didn't push her away. I made it clear that I didn't want anything to happen between us. She understood my reservations.

Layla laid her head on my shoulder then wrapped her arm around my waist. "There's nothing wrong with cuddling, right?"

"I guess not," I whispered.

"Good."

When the movie was over, I looked at Layla. She was asleep. I picked her up then carried her into my bedroom, placing her on my bed. After I shut the door, I lay on the couch and tried to fall asleep. I kept thinking about Elisa. It broke my heart that I wouldn't see her again for over a year, but my heart broke even more when I thought about seeing her. It was a catch-22. She would probably be hurt that I didn't say goodbye, but I didn't have a choice. It had to be done.

I went to work the next morning and walked into my boss' office. He and I were somewhat close. We spent time outside of work golfing at the country club and playing tennis at the gym. He always liked me as a worker and I always like him as a boss. I didn't have any complaints.

"Good morning, sir," I said as I shook his hand.

"Hello, Mr. Montague. What can I do for you?"

"I need to talk to you about something."

"Is it about the Christmas bonus? I've heard the rumors going on around the office," he said with a smile. "And to answer your question, yes it's true."

I laughed. "Thank you. That's very generous of you. But I actually wanted to discuss something else."

"And what would that be?"

"Well, I recently found out that I have to move to London. I'm here to submit my two weeks."

He sat forward, his eyes wide. "What? What's in London?"

I felt bad for lying but I knew I had to. "My mother. She's sick."

"Oh. I had no idea."

"Yeah. She needs someone to care of her and I'm all she has. I don't know how much longer she has."

"That's horrible."

"Yeah."

He said nothing for a long time. "I hate to lose you, Jared, but I understand that I have to let you go."

"Thank you, sir."

"And forget about the formality. You can leave anytime you want."

"I really appreciate that."

"You're welcome. Are you going to be living in London indefinitely?"

"No. I intend to return after—you know."

He nodded. "Well, your job will be waiting for you if you decide to come back."

I was moved by the gesture. There were thousands of applications that were submitted every day. That was the most generous offer I had ever received. "Thank you so much, sir. That means a lot to me."

"Of course. And you have my condolences, Jared. I'm sorry that you have to deal with this."

"Thank you."

"So, when do you leave?"

"If you're sure it's okay, I'll leave tomorrow."

"I wish you well."

"I actually have another favor to ask."

"What is it?"

"Could you keep my situation to yourself and not tell the rest of the office? At least until after I'm gone. I just don't want people to pity me."

"Of course. I won't say anything. I completely understand. Real men don't want people's pity or remorse. You're above that, Jared."

I nodded. "Yeah."

My boss stood up and extended his hand. I shook it.

"Good luck, Jared."

"Thank you, sir. You too."

"And Merry Christmas."

"Merry Christmas."

I left the office and closed the door behind me. I walked by Ethan's office on the way back to mine. He hadn't spoken to me since he saw me at the house. I'm surprised he hadn't threatened me or questioned me. Elisa hadn't called me either. I wondered if she had given up. She said she never would.

When the work day was over, I waited for everyone to leave before I packed my desk in a box then left the office. I wanted to be discreet about my departure, especially to Ethan. If he knew I was leaving, he would question me or tell Elisa about my plans to leave. I had to keep it a secret if I was really going to escape.

When I got back to the apartment, Layla was still there.

"How was your last day?"

"It was okay."

"So, you wanna go out to celebrate?"

"To celebrate what?"

She shrugged. "Your last night here?"

"I guess."

"Where do you want to go?"

"Somewhere quiet. That café was fine."

She rolled her eyes. "You know how to live it up, huh?"

I laughed. "I'm just too depressed to be happy."

She looked at me with saddened eyes. "I know."

After I showered, we left the apartment and grabbed coffee at the café. We sat by the window while I picked at my deli sandwich. I wasn't hungry. I hadn't been hungry in a long time. Layla stared at me for a while without saying anything. She respected my silence.

"How long will you be in London?" I asked.

"Just a few days. Then I have to get back to work."

I nodded. "Well, at least I'll have one friend while I'm there."

"And I'm always a phone call away." She placed her hand on top of mine and caressed my knuckles. I didn't mind her affection. Her touch didn't ignite me like Elisa's did. It was more of a dull ache. I didn't think I would ever feel that intense heat again. With Elisa, I felt so hot I thought I would explode. In comparison, Layla felt like a sister. It was amazing how much Elisa had captured my heart. She had it the moment I saw her. I was drawn to her like the flowers lean toward the sun.

The door of the café opened and I felt my heart fall when I saw Ethan. He was staring right at me, a look of pure rage on his face. I knew this wasn't going to be good. I quickly pulled my hand away. I knew this looked bad.

Ethan marched toward me, his arms swinging at his sides. I knew he was going to yell and scream at me in the middle of the café. I had nowhere to run and nowhere to hide.

When his fist collided with my face, I fell back into my chair. I was not expecting him to hit me, especially in a public place.

"You're such a piece of shit!" He punched me again.

I held up my hand. "What the hell is your problem?"

"So you fuck my sister after you dump her, break her heart again, then fuck with this tramp a few days later?" He threw another punch at me but I grabbed it and pushed him back. I was sick of Ethan's bullshit. I rose from the chair and stared him down. I had been taking my boxing and self-defense classes for a long time and was eager to use them. Everyone in the café moved away from us. I saw the cashier pick up the phone, probably calling the cops.

"I'm sick of your bullshit, Ethan. I didn't fuck your sister then just leave. Why don't you ask her what happened? She tricked me—*tricked me*. The last thing I would ever want to do is hurt her. And not that it's any of your business, but I'm not sleeping with this woman. She's just my friend."

"Liar," Ethan said as he threw another punch.

I grabbed his first then hit him on the arm, making him retract it with a groan. I punched him across the face, making his nose bleed, then stepped back, waiting for him to hit me again. When he aimed for my face, I grabbed him arm, pinned it behind his back, then kicked his knees from under him, sending him to the floor. I pressed my knees again his back. "Elisa is the one who broke my heart—not the other way around." I pulled his arm back so it would hurt. "I'm tired of being threatened by you all the time. How would you feel if my sister threatened to hurt Elisa for all the shit she's done to me?" Ethan said nothing. "I didn't want to be at the house the other day. She came to my apartment in the middle of the night and I had to drag her home. She begged me to stay with her. I set my alarm to

166

leave before everyone woke up, but she disabled it so I would have to spend time with the kids." I released his hands and stepped away, knowing he wouldn't fight me again. "She and I are done. Don't worry. You'll never have to see me again." I grabbed Layla by the arm then led her to the front door. I needed to get away before I hit him again.

"I'm sorry about that," I said as I guided her up the street.

She used her sleeve to wipe my nose. I was still bleeding. "Are you okay?"

"Yeah, I'm fine."

"That was uncalled for."

"He's always been that way with Elisa. I understand it but it's really pissing me off. She is the one who broke my heart—not the other way around. And it pisses me off that my sister doesn't do shit about it."

"Talk to her."

"I shouldn't have to."

When we got back to the apartment, I cleaned myself up and finished packing all my essentials. I was leaving for airport late that evening. The flight was eight hours so we would land by the next night in their time zone.

I picked up my phone and called Alex. "Can you come over?"

"Uh, sure. Hi, by the way."

"Yeah whatever. Can you come by?"

"I'm on my way." I hung up.

"Who's that?" Layla asked.

"My friend Alex."

"Are you going to say goodbye?"

"I have something to give him."

"Oh."

A few minutes later, Alex arrived.

When he walked in, his eyes widened. "What the fuck is going on? Are you moving?"

"Yeah."

"What? Why didn't you tell me?"

"I'm telling you now."

"Where are you going?"

"London."

"What the fuck?"

"Just shut up."

"Is this because of Elisa?"

"What do you think?"

"You're insane."

"I don't refute that."

Layla came over and shook Alex's hand. "Hi. I'm Layla."

"Uh," he stumbled as he looked at her. "Hi. I'm Alex." He looked at her for a long moment before he turned back to me.

I grabbed two envelopes sitting on the counter. "I need you to give these to Sadie."

He looked at them. "And Elisa?"

"Sadie will give it to her."

"You aren't going to tell your sister you're moving?" he asked incredulously.

"What do you think the letter is for?"

"That's cowardly."

"She'll try to stop me if I tell her beforehand. I'm about to leave for the airport and I'm turning my phone off.

No matter how fast you get that to her, it will be too late. I'll already be gone."

He was quiet for a moment. "When are you coming back?"

"A year or two."

"She ruined you."

"Yeah."

He sighed. "I don't suppose I can change your mind?"

I smiled. "No."

"Well, I'll miss you, man."

"Yeah. I'll miss you too."

"I don't know what to say."

I wrapped my arms around him and hugged him for a second. "I'll be back before you know it."

"Yeah," he said as he pulled away.

"Take care."

He nodded. I could tell how upset he was just by looking at him. I was glad I didn't have to see the same look on Sadie and Elisa's faces.

"Well, this is it," I said. I grabbed a few bags and Layla grabbed the rest. We walked out the door then shut it. I slid the key underneath. I stared at the closed door for a moment. I'll never set foot in that apartment again. "Okay."

Layla smiled at me, trying to assuage my fear.

We walked down to the street and hailed a cab. Alex watched us climb inside. He stayed on the sidewalk until we started to pull away. I held up a hand and waved. He nodded back. The car drove down the road and took us to JFK airport. I pulled out my phone then turned it off. It would only be a matter of time before it started to ring like crazy. Layla grabbed my hand and squeezed it, understanding how hard this was for me.

When we arrived at the airport, we checked in and got our luggage on board. I stared at my ticket while we waited for the flight attendant to usher us onto the plane. It said it was a one way flight. That made my heart accelerate. I was really doing this.

When our flight was called, I didn't move.

"Come on," Layla said as she grabbed my hand. "It's okay."

I took a deep breath. This was harder than I thought it was going to be. I could just go back to Elisa and give her another chance, but I knew that would be a mistake. I would miss my sister's wedding but I felt like she didn't care about me anyway. My dad wouldn't know anything until it was too late.

I finally rose to my feet. "Okay."

"You're going to be alright, Jared."

I said nothing. I turned to the counter and handed my ticket to the clerk.

"Have a wonderful flight, Mr. Montague."

I nodded then boarded the plane.

# 17

London was beautiful—freezing—but beautiful. My mother was ecstatic that I decided to move there spontaneously. It was so different from New York that I couldn't even describe it. Even though the citizens still spoke English, I could barely understand them most of the time. Their accents could be so thick.

Layla showed me a few of the tourist spots as well as the better pubs she had been to. Even though nothing reminded me of Elisa, I still thought of her. Just an ad on the side of the cab was enough to make me think about her. If anything, I always thought of her until something distracted me. When the distraction was gone, my thoughts returned to her.

The biggest issue I had with London was the streets. The cars drove on the opposite side of the road and there were a lot of smaller one way streets. I almost got hit by cars a few times. Layla didn't introduce me to her family but she introduced me to a few friends she had in the city. They were nice—difficult to understand—but nice.

Layla didn't stay with me at my mom's house. She stayed with her uncle a few streets away. I didn't want my mom to assume that Layla was anything more than a friend. I wasn't sure why Layla was so nice to me. I knew she was attracted to me and was interested in me, but I was an emotional wreck with a bunch of baggage. She would always be second best and she understood that. The revelation reminded me of myself. I was the same way with Elisa.

We went to the theatre one night and watched a play. Layla held my hand while we watched the show but I didn't pull away. As long as she didn't try to kiss me or seduce me, I was fine with it. And I wasn't sure what her affection even meant—friendly or romantic. I assumed it was friendly since I was in so much pain. I wish I could just forget about Elisa and fall for Layla. I could tell the girl wouldn't hurt me. She was a bit obsessed with me, really.

I still hadn't turned on my phone because I didn't want to deal with all the questions, emotions, and utter turmoil. My sister realized I was with our mom so she called her a few times. Every time my mom tried to get me on the phone, I left the townhouse. I knew my sister was pissed at me because of what I wrote in her letter. I basically told her she cared more about Ethan than me, and she didn't give a shit about me whatsoever. She let her boyfriend disrespect me on a daily basis when her sister-in-law turned out to be the heartbreaker. I was pissed at Sadie. I didn't care how mad she was. That's how I really felt—like I didn't matter.

I had dinner with my mom almost every evening. My mom's boyfriend hadn't come around yet. I wasn't sure if I should be relieved or not. If I liked the guy, it would be a betrayal to my father, but if I didn't like the guy, it would cause me trouble since he was my boss in a way.

I stabbed my broccoli with my fork while I ate at the kitchen table. I hadn't seen my mom in seven years so it was difficult to become accustomed to her presence again.

"So, how are you liking it?" she asked.

"It's beautiful."

She smiled. "Now you know why I moved here. Americans are a bunch of rude idiots."

"Mom, you're American."

"Yep."

I smiled. "Well, at least you realize it."

"But don't tell anyone that you're American."

"They are going to figure it out by my accent."

"Then speak in a British one."

I rolled my eyes. "I'm not doing that."

"It will happen eventually."

I chewed my broccoli and ignored her comment.

"So why are you here, Jared?"

"I—I just wanted to leave the city."

"I thought you loved it there."

"I did."

"And what changed?"

I shrugged. "I just didn't like it anymore."

"Does this have anything to do with a girl?"

My mom and I were never close and we weren't going to start now. "No."

"You're a horrible liar. You make the same face your father makes."

I averted my gaze. "I don't want to talk about it."

"Okay."

I raised an eyebrow. That was it? She wasn't going to pester me.

"What?"

"You're not going to try to pull it out of me?"

She shook her head. "You're an adult. It's none of my business unless you want it to be."

"Thanks."

"So, who's that girl you're always with?"

"My friend, Layla."

"Is she from New York?"

"Yeah. She's just helping me get settled."

"That's very nice of her."

"Yeah."

"And she's going to leave?"

"Yeah."

"Hmm."

"What?"

"You don't like her? She's very beautiful."

"We're just friends," I said quickly.

"I can't imagine what this other girl must have looked like, then. She must have been truly exceptional."

She was but I would never say that. There was an awkward silence that passed between us. My chewing became amplified in my ears.

"How's work?"

"It's good."

"You like it?"

I shrugged. "It's fine. It's a job."

"Roger says everyone loves you already."

"Well, that's good."

"You must be a lot more charming at work than at home," she said with a smile.

"I'm sorry. I'm just not myself lately."

"I understand."

I drank from my glass of water then returned it to the table.

"So, how's Sadie?"

"She's good."

"Anything new with her?"

I didn't know what to say. I wasn't sure if Sadie was planning on telling her that she was engaged. I knew she didn't want her there. "Uh, no." I was pissed at my sister but I would still cover her ass.

"And your father?"

"Why do you ask if you don't really care?" I snapped.

Her eyes widened. "I do care."

I didn't meet her gaze and continued to eat.

"Jared, our divorce was the greatest thing that happened to both of us. He and I are both happy. I still love and respect him."

I knew my dad wasn't happy. He was lonely. I spent as much time with him as I could but it was never enough. And he never moved on because he still loved my mom, for whatever reason.

I pushed my plate away. "I'm going to bed."

"Jared?"

"What?" I placed my plate in the sink.

"I'm always here if you need to talk."

"I know, Mom."

"Good night, baby."

"Night."

When I went into my bedroom, I finally turned on my phone. My message box was full. I didn't feel like listening to any of them. I was glad it couldn't hold any more messages. I wished I could just delete them without listening to them.

I called Layla. "Hey."

"Hey."

"What time do you leave tomorrow?"

"In the morning."

"Oh."

"You sad to see me go?"

"Yeah," I said with a smile.

"I'll be back soon."

"You can't stay for Christmas?"

"No. The holidays are the busiest time of year for us."

I laughed. "That makes sense."

"We can still Skype."

"I would like that."

"Or you could you just come home with me."

"You know I can't do that."

"Have you talked to anyone?"

"No. My message box is full so they must be eager to get a hold of me."

"Yikes. That's going to take a while to go through."

"Yeah."

"Has your mom talked to them?"

"Sadie calls every day."

"And what does she say?"

"I don't know. I always leave the house."

"You can't avoid her forever."

"I know. I just want them to accept the fact that I'm staying."

"It sounds like you're afraid she'll convince you to come home."

"Maybe."

She yawned. "Well, I should go to bed."

"Me too."

"Are you coming to the airport with me?"

"Yeah. I'll go before work."

"Okay. I'll see you then."

"Bye."

I hung up then turned off my phone again. I stared at the ceiling, unable to think about anything but Elisa. Did I make a mistake going there? If I was so in love with her, why shouldn't I just be with her? Maybe I should give her another chance. But then the doubt came back. I had to stay strong. She would just hurt me over and over again. I had to stay strong.

Perhaps I was more depressed because Christmas was coming. I fantasized about waking up with Elisa in my arms then making love to her quietly. The kids would come to the door and demand to open gifts. We could sit under the tree, drinking hot cocoa as we watched their eyes light up in joy. When the tears burned my eyes, I closed them and started to count to a hundred. When I reached the eighties, I fell asleep.

# 18

I took Layla to the airport the next morning. I walked with her as far as I could go without a ticket. She and I stood together until her flight was called. We didn't talk about anything important, just random things that came to mind. She stared at me the whole time with pity in her eyes.

"Have a safe trip back."

"I would call you but your phone will probably be off."

I smiled. "I'll turn it on when I get back."

"And leave it on. It's been a few days. It's time to deal with it, Jared."

"You're right."

"Obviously."

"Don't get cocky."

"Too late."

I smiled at her. "Thanks for coming with me."

"No problem. What are friends for?"

"I'll miss you."

"I'll miss you too." She wrapped her arms around my neck and hugged me. When she pulled away, she placed her lips over mine in a gentle kiss. Initially, I was immobile, but I responded to her affection a second later. I wasn't thinking. It just happened. It was soft and wet. When she pulled away, she smiled at me. "That will have to hold me over until the next time I see you."

I didn't say anything.

"Jared, you're mine as soon as you're ready."

"Why do you like me so much?"

"Sometimes you just know." She turned around and walked toward the gate. I watched her with a sad expression. An amazing girl loved me and I didn't feel the same way. I hated this. I wished that Elisa didn't hurt me, or that I was over her. I didn't think I would ever be over her. I loved her like crazy. I wanted to punch something.

I left the airport then took a cab to work. It was quiet around the building. I stayed in my office and worked throughout the day. Every once in a while, I would open my wallet and stare at the picture of Becky and Tommy. When the emotion overcame me, I closed it and returned to my pocket. I needed to stop doing that. It was just making me sadder. I went there to stop thinking about her, not to stare at pictures of her kids—my kids.

There was a knock on my door. "Come in."

A tall man came inside. He had brown hair and a strong frame. Even though he was in his forties, he looked healthy and strong. "Hello, Mr. Montague. I'm sorry I haven't come by sooner. Been rather busy." He had a strong British accent. "I'm Roger."

I stood up and shook his hand. "It's nice to meet you. Thank you for the wonderful opportunity."

"Well, you've been a great worker so far. I'm glad that your mother recommended you."

I smiled. "My mom exaggerates my qualities sometimes."

He laughed. "Don't all mothers?"

I nodded. "True."

"Do you have any questions or concerns? Anything I can help you with?"

"No. I got it figured out. But thank you for the offer."

"So, your mom tells me you have a sister. What's she like?"

I opened my wallet and showed him a picture. "She's an annoying pain. That's about it."

He laughed as he looked at the picture. "Beautiful girl. She looks like your mother."

I shrugged. "I try not to let it go to her head."

He smiled. "Let's have lunch this afternoon. I would like to get to know you better."

I felt like I would betray my father if I spent time with my mother's lover, but I couldn't turn the guy down, especially since he got me the job. Also, he was really nice. "That sounds great."

"Wonderful," he said as he clapped his hands. "Let's go at noon."

"I look forward to it, sir."

He nodded. "Call me Roger."

"Will do."

He left my office then disappeared down the hallway. I concentrated on my work until lunchtime came around. Roger appeared at my office door right on the hour.

"Ready to go, Jared?"

"Yes," I said as I rose from my desk. I saved my document then followed him out the door.

"So what sounds good?"

"I'm not a picky eater."

He laughed. "I'm glad you aren't too similar to your mother."

"For Thanksgiving every year, she would only eat a salad and a side of beets."

"She's a bit odd."

"A bit?"

He laughed. "But I love that woman."

His declaration made me uncomfortable. I was still on my dad's side.

"How about the deli?"

"I like sandwiches."

We crossed the street and entered the small shop. They had an assortment of sandwiches and a collection of teas. When I tried to pay for my food, Roger put the cash on the table and paid for both of us. Now I felt like he was kissing my ass. I didn't like it.

We sat down at a table by the window. He sipped his tea while he ate his lunch. The weather outside was gray and cold. I hadn't seen the sun once since I had been there. The city was beautiful, but dark and ugly at the same time. I guess I was just spoiled with the moderate snow of New York City.

"So do you have a woman in your life?" he asked.

"No."

He nodded. "You're a good looking guy. You'll find the right one easily."

I said nothing. I hated talking about my love life with people, especially people I hardly knew.

"I'm impressed that you went to Harvard. I feel like I already know you. Your mother never stops talking about you two."

"Really?" I blurted. It didn't seem like she cared for me or Sadie.

"Yes. She always says how much she misses you. She always wants to visit but she's afraid you don't want her to."

"She never told me that."

"Perhaps I shouldn't have said anything."

I chewed my bite of sandwich and looked out the window.

"I'm really glad you're here, Jared. Your mother was so excited when she told me you were coming. I don't think she'll ever let you leave the house."

"Then I'll have to sneak out."

"You very well may have to," he said. "I don't have any kids of my own but now I wish I did."

"Have you been married?"

"Once. She passed away a long time ago."

"Oh, I'm sorry."

"It's okay. It took me a long time to get over it but I did eventually."

I leaned back in my chair then wiped my mouth with a napkin.

"I'm thinking about asking your mother to marry me."

"What?"

"You sound surprised."

"I just can't see her getting married. She's had a different boyfriend every year."

He smiled. "Perhaps I'm the right one that can tame her."

I said nothing. I didn't know my mother well enough to say what she wanted.

"So, how do you feel about that?"

"What do you mean?"

"About me marrying your mother?"

I shrugged. "I don't know. It's her life. She can make her own choices and decisions without my consent or approval. It wouldn't make a difference if she gave me hers when I got married."

"Sometimes people are uncomfortable when their parents get remarried. That's all I was asking."

"My parents have been divorced for seven years. That's plenty of time for me to accept it."

He nodded. "So I have your blessing to ask?"

"Of course. I want my mom to be happy."

"Thank you. That's all I wanted."

We finished our meal then returned to work. When I was back in the office, I thought about the conversation we just had. Even though I felt like I was betraying my dad, I realized it didn't make a difference. My mother would remarry anyway, and my dad was better off without her. She didn't love him so it really didn't matter.

When my work day was finally over, I went to the pub and had a beer before I walked home to the townhouse my mom owned. It was nice because it was right in the midst of the city. I didn't mind walking but I still wasn't used to the chilling cold. It was even more bitter than winter in Manhattan.

When I walked inside, my mother looked at me. She was on the phone.

"Okay. He's right here."

I held up my hand, knowing it was Sadie, and turned away.

"Jared!" she yelled. "This is important. Something has happened."

I stopped and looked at her. "What?"

She held the phone to me. "Talk to your sister."

I pushed it away. "No. You can tell me."

"Jared, just talk to her. Please."

After I stared at the fear in her eyes, I took the phone and held it up to my ear. I didn't say anything for a long time. I heard Sadie whimpering. I knew she was crying. I'm sure she wanted to apologize for everything and beg me to come home. I didn't want to listen to it.

"What?" I snapped.

"Jared?"

"Get on with it."

She stared to cry harder. "It's Elisa."

My heart fell. "What? What happened? Tell me. Is she okay? What's going on?"

She started to mumble incoherently through her tears.

"SADIE! Speak up!"

"She's in the hospital."

I started to hyperventilate. "Is she okay? What happened?"

My mom covered her face while she watched me.

"She was mugged then beaten. Someone took her to the hospital. We just got here."

I felt the walls cave in. This couldn't be happening. I couldn't take it. "Is she okay? Is she alive?"

"I think so."

"*You think so?* Tell me!"

"I'll tell you everything as soon as I find out."

"The kids, are they okay?"

"They're fine."

"Were they there?"

"No."

"Ethan?"

"He wasn't there."

"Then what the fuck happened?"

"I don't want to say."

"TELL ME!"

They found her near your building," she whispered. "We think she was looking for you, hoping you were still in the city."

Tears fell down my face. "She went out by herself in the middle of the night?"

"Yeah."

"Fuck." The tears kept falling. "This is all my fault."

"Are you coming?"

I wiped my tears away. "I'm leaving now."

"Okay."

I dropped the phone on the floor. I stared at my mother but didn't really look at her. My mind was racing with the speed of light. I dashed upstairs and grabbed all my stuff then headed to the front door.

"You're leaving?" she asked.

"Yes."

"But what about your job?"

"I don't care."

"Wait until the weekend. There's nothing you can do for her."

"Bye." I slammed the door behind me then jumped in a cab. I told the driver to take me to the airport. I stared at the wet streets and thought about Elisa. I couldn't believe this was happening. If I had said goodbye before I left, she wouldn't have looked for me. If I just answered my phone, I could have spared her. I loved her so much, and now she's in the hospital because of me. She must have been so scared. I should have been the one protecting her. I failed her and the kids. I just wanted to die.

# 19

The next twelve hours were agonizing. I had to wait to catch a flight, and when I finally got on one it was delayed. I was wound up so tight that I could've killed someone. My legs wouldn't stop shaking as I waited and waited. When the plane finally took off, I was stuck in a chair for eight hours, suffocated by the thoughts of Elisa. Her brother was going to kill me when he saw me, but I didn't care. I deserved the beating of a lifetime.

When the plane finally landed, I practically pushed an old lady out of the way just so I could get off the plane as fast as I could. I grabbed my luggage from the collection stand then whistled down a cab. That drive felt just as long as the plane. When the hospital came into sight, I jumped out of the halted cab, forgetting to pay the driver and grab my luggage.

When the cab driver caught my attention, I threw a fifty at him then grabbed my bags and dashed to the entrance.

"Elisa Benedict. I'm looking for Elisa Benedict," I said, out of breath.

The receptionist stared at me for a moment before she looked in her computer. "There's no one here under that name."

"Yes, there is! Check again!"

She leaned back at my ferocity.

"Please check," I said hysterically.

She looked again. "I'm sorry, sir."

I screamed.

"Jared!"

I turned to see Sadie looking at me. "Come on."

I raised an eyebrow then followed her. "Where is she? How is she? Is she okay?"

"She's fine," she said as she grabbed my arm. "Keep your voice down and stop yelling."

We entered a small private room. I dropped my bags on the ground then went to the bed. She was lying there, asleep. Her face was purple and bruised. She had a cut on her lip and her arms were dark with bruises.

I broke down. "No, no."

I leaned over her and pressed my forehead against hers. "I'm so sorry, Ellie. I'm so sorry." I kissed her forehead and tasted my own tears. I grabbed her hand and held it tightly. When she didn't wake up, I got scared. "Ellie, wake up. Please wake up."

"Jared," Sadie said. "Let her sleep."

"Why isn't she waking up?"

She stared at me. "She hasn't woken up yet."

"What?"

"She hit her head."

I sat up and looked at her. "Are you telling me she's in a coma?"

"No. She just hasn't woken up yet. Don't try to wake her."

I sat on the edge of the bed and held her hand. I stared at her face and felt my world crumble. "Where are the kids?"

"Ethan has them."

"Do they know?"

"No. We don't want them to know. They think she's out shopping."

"For a few days?"

"The kids believe it. That's all that matters."

I ran my fingers through my hair. "I'm so sorry. Fuck, I'm sorry."

"It's not your fault."

"Shut up. Yes, it is."

"Jared, no, it's not."

I didn't respond to her comment. "Did they catch the bastard?"

"No. She needs to give a description when she wakes up."

I sighed. "I'll find him."

She said nothing.

"Did anything else—happen?"

"No."

I swallowed the lump in my throat. "Thank god." I would die if someone raped her. I really couldn't stand the thought.

Sadie stared at me but said nothing.

I held Elisa's hand within mine and felt her pulse. It made me feel better because it was strong. She was going to be okay. She was going to be okay.

"Jared—"

"No," I interrupted her. "Drop it." I knew what she was going to say. She wanted to talk about the letter. "Now isn't the best time," I snapped.

"I just wanted to say I'm sorry, Jared. That's all."

I said nothing.

The nurse came in. "Visiting hours are over. You can come back in the morning."

"You may as well call security because I'm not going anywhere," I said as I looked at Elisa. "And I won't go quietly."

Sadie looked at me. "Jared—"

"I mean it," I snapped.

The nurse sighed. "It's not worth it. He can stay."

Sadie nodded. "Thank you."

The nurse left.

Sadie grabbed my bags from the floor. "I'll take these home."

I didn't say anything.

Sadie came behind me then wrapped her arms around my torso. I didn't reciprocate her embrace at all. My hands were still on Elisa.

"I love you," she whispered.

I remained silent.

"I'll see you tomorrow," she said as she released me. She walked out and closed the door behind her.

The only light in the room was from the monitor by her bed side. I grabbed a chair and pulled it next to her bed. I held her hand as I laid my head beside hers. I listened to her breathing until my eyes grew heavy. I closed them and fell asleep.

When the door opened a moment later, or it seemed like a moment, I sat up and rubbed the sleep from eyes.

"Good morning," a man in a white coat said.

I said nothing.

"That's gonna hurt later today," he said as he looked at my neck. He sat on the stool then observed Elisa, checking her vital signs and her IV. He examined her bruises and cuts. "Well, the CT came back this morning."

"And?"

"She doesn't have any permanent brain damage. She's just recovering from the trauma."

"She's going to be okay?"

"Yes. She can leave when she wakes up."

I breathed a sigh of relief. "Thank god."

"Are you Mrs. Wyatt's husband?"

"Who?"

He stared at the chart. "Elisa's husband?"

"Oh—uh—no. Her boyfriend. She's a widow."

He nodded. "My apologies."

"Yeah."

He left the room, closing the door behind him.

Now I understood why the receptionist couldn't find her. She still had her husband's last name—not Ethan's. I ran my fingers through her hair and stared at her face. The bruises pained my heart. She must have been so scared. I wished this hadn't happened to her. I sat vigil next to her for hours before there was a knock on the door.

Ethan walked into the room. He didn't look surprised to see me.

"I'm not leaving," I blurted. "So save it."

He sat in the chair on the opposite side of the room. "I wasn't going to ask you to."

"Good," I snapped.

"Any news?"

"Doctor says she doesn't have any brain damage."

Ethan breathed a sigh of relief. "Oh, thank god." Tears bubbled under his eyes but he blinked them back.

"How are the kids?"

"Oblivious."

I nodded.

"Sadie is watching them."

"Okay."

I squeezed Elisa's hand. I hadn't drop it since I got there. I wanted her to know I was there even if she couldn't speak or see. "I'm sorry," I whispered.

Ethan looked at me. "It isn't your fault."

I stared at him, incredulous. "It's completely my fault. I shouldn't have left, or I should have told her I was really leaving. She obviously thought I was lying or was still at the apartment. If I just answered my phone, I could have stopped this."

He sighed. "Don't beat up yourself over it. It was my fault too. I should have heard her leave."

A tear fell down my face. "I'm so sorry."

"It's okay."

"No, it's not. No."

Ethan fell silent.

I cried quietly to myself, hating myself for it. This was entirely my fault. "You should kill me."

"It's not your fault," he repeated.

"So, the one time I actually do something wrong, you don't care? But I get punched for crimes I didn't commit?"

"I was wrong to hit you before, but you didn't do anything wrong here. Let it go. She's going to be okay. That's all that matters at this point."

I shook my head. "I can't believe you. If something happened to Sadie, I would hold you responsible for it."

"That's completely different and you know it."

I said nothing.

"Jared, no one holds you responsible. She went out on her own."

"Shut up," I snapped.

He fell silent.

I grabbed her hand and kissed it.

We sat together for a long time. Only the sound of the monitor could be heard. I stared at Elisa and watched her breathe. The IV machine would beep every once in a while. It was a nice distraction.

When I saw her eyes flutter open, I felt my heart race. The tears poured down my face. I didn't move or speak because I didn't want to scare her. Her last memory must have been horrific. When her eyes were completely open, she stared at me for a long time until she recognized me.

"Jared?" she said with a croak.

"Yeah," I whispered.

She reached her hand toward mine. Instead, I leaned over and pressed my forehead against hers. She wrapped her arms around my neck and squeezed me tightly.

"I'm so sorry," I sobbed. "I'm so sorry."

She said nothing while she held me.

"Ellie, I love you. I love you so much."

"I love you too," she whispered.

"You are everything to me. I'm so sorry."

"It's okay. I'm okay."

I kissed her forehead then her cheeks. "I didn't know what I would do if—"

"Shh."

"I'm sorry," I sobbed.

"It's not your fault, Jared."

"Yes, it is. I'm supposed to protect you. I failed."

"Jared, calm down."

I took a deep breath. "I'm sorry. You're right. I'm so glad you're okay. I'm so grateful." I pulled away and looked down at her. "How are you feeling? Are you in pain?"

"A little."

"I'll get the nurse."

She grabbed me. "No. Don't go."

"Okay."

She placed her hand on my chest and gently rubbed me. "You didn't have to come, Jared."

"I love you. Of course I had to."

"I'm not your responsibility anymore."

"Shut up. You're always my responsibility. I love you."

Her eyes softened but she said nothing.

Ethan stood up then approached the bed. "Hey," he whispered.

She turned to him. "Ethan?"

"Hey." He wrapped his arms around her and hugged her tightly. He started to cry quietly. "I'm so glad you're okay."

"I know."

"I love you so much."

"I love you too."

He continued to hold her while the tears fell down his face.

"Where are my babies?"

"They're at home with Sadie."

"Do they—know?" she asked.

"No. They have no idea."

"Good."

He rubbed her back while he held her. I looked away to give them some privacy. When Ethan finally pulled away, his eyes were still red. He wiped them and looked at his sister. "It's going to be okay."

"I know," she whispered.

"The doctor said you're going to be fine. He said you could go home."

She breathed a sigh of relief. "Good."

"You still need to give a description of the mugger before we go," he said quietly.

Her eyes widened in fear. "No."

"Elisa—"

"No." She started to cry. "I can't—no."

I grabbed her face and kissed her gently. Her cries were stifled for a moment. "Ellie, please do this for me. I'll be here the whole time—both of us."

"I can't."

"Yes, you can. Please."

She kept crying.

I kissed her tears away and ran my fingers through her hair. "Calm down."

"I'm trying," she said between breaths.

"It's okay, it's okay."

"Okay," she said.

"Please do this for me."

She was quiet for a long time. "Okay."

"Thank you."

195

Ethan rose from the bed. "I'll be right back."

I kept Elisa's face close to mine. We stared at each other for a long time, neither one of us saying anything. When she looked into my eyes, she seemed to feel calm, distracted. I wanted her to stay that way, so I ran my fingers through her hair gently. Her eyes were still red but the tears stopped falling. I wanted to ask her what happened but I couldn't. It would make her hysterical again.

Ethan returned a moment later with two police officers behind him.

Elisa immediately grabbed my hand. I sat beside her on the bed then wrapped my arm around her shoulder, holding her close to me. My fingers glided gently over her skin.

"Elisa Wyatt?" the first office asked. He was short and broad. He didn't look like he could run fast, but it seemed like he could throw a punch with massive force. He had brown hair that matched his eyes.

She cleared her throat. "Yes."

"Can you describe the attacker?"

The other police officer opened a pad of paper and placed the tip of the pencil to the paper.

"Uh, yeah," she said.

I rubbed her back. "Come on, Ellie."

"He had brown hair."

"Short or long?" the officer asked.

"Medium," she answered. "It's the same length as my brother's."

The artist glanced at Ethan and started to scribble.

She continued. "He's taller than me—the same height as Jared. His eyes reached my forehead."

196

"I'm six foot," I said.

The artist nodded.

The police officer looked at Elisa. "Weight?"

"Uh, I don't know. He was big."

"Fat, chubby, muscular?"

"No. Skinny but big."

"And what does that mean?" the office asked with a roll of his eyes.

I glared at him. "I suggest you show some respect. I have no problem calling your supervisor and giving a full report on your obvious disrespect and inability to do your job right. Knock it off." Elisa flinched beside me. "My girlfriend just experienced a major trauma. If you don't give a shit, then you shouldn't be here. You got it?"

The officer stared at me for a moment before he looked at Elisa. "Please describe him in more detail."

"That's better," I snapped.

"Uh, he was thin and toned. Like a soccer player."

"You're doing great, baby," I whispered.

The artist continued to scribble.

"Any distinguishable features?" he asked.

"He had a beard and a freckle on one eyelid."

"Which one?" the officer asked.

"The left one," she answered.

"Race?"

"White."

He nodded. "Anything else you think we should know?"

"He had a knife," she answered.

"Thank you," he said. "Can you tell us what happened?"

197

She started to shake.

"It's okay," I whispered in her ear. "It's okay."

She took a deep breath. "Before I reached the building, he came from nowhere. It was dark. I don't really know." She paused and held me tighter. "He pushed me against the wall and held a knife to my throat. Then he demanded that I hand over everything I had. I was so scared that I didn't move. That's when he started to hit me." I closed my eyes, unable to take it anymore. It was too painful. "He hit me until I fell to the ground then he kicked me. When I covered my face, he pulled everything from my pocket and took my purse. He kicked me in the head and that's the last thing I remember."

I brought her close to me and rested my head on top of hers. I didn't want her to see me cry. Her story was too painful to imagine. Knowing she was beaten like that broke my heart into thousands of pieces. She was shaking and I held her close.

"I think we have everything," the officer said.

The artist stepped toward us and showed us the drawing. "Is this him?"

We stared at it for a moment then she nodded.

"Thank you," he said.

Both of the officers left.

"You did great, Ellie," I whispered.

She didn't say anything.

Hours later, the nurse came into the room and started to unhook her IV. "You're free to go."

"Thank you," she whispered.

"Of course, honey," she said. "And here are your clothes." She placed the plastic bag on the end of the bed. Then she left.

Elisa tried to stand up but I pushed her back.

"Let me help you."

"I can do it," she said.

Ethan looked uncomfortable. "I'll be outside." He got up and left.

I grabbed the clothes and cringed when I saw the dry blood. I tried to ignore it and helped her get dressed. It was either that or she would have to wear my clothes. As I stripped off her gown, I saw the discoloration along her ribs. She was bruised badly.

"It doesn't hurt," she said quickly.

I knew she was lying. I helped her get dressed then gathered her in my arms.

"I can walk. My legs don't hurt."

"I got you."

She wrapped her arms around my neck and didn't argue.

We joined Ethan in the hall then left the hospital, getting in a cab off the street. While we drove back to the townhouse, I placed my arm around her shoulder and held her close. No one said anything on the ride home.

When we arrived at the house, Ethan looked at his sister. "How do we explain this to the kids?"

"Uh, I don't know."

She had bruises on her face. It was hard to hide. They would be there for several weeks.

"I'll just say I fell down or something," she whispered.

I couldn't think of a better idea. Judging by Ethan's blank expression, he didn't have a better idea either.

We climbed out of the cab then came to the front door. Ethan unlocked it and we all walked inside. As soon as we entered the living room, the kids ran toward us. They stopped when they saw Elisa.

"Mommy?" Tommy asked. "Are you hurt?"

She kneeled down and hugged him tightly. "No. I just had an accident."

Becky came over and pointed at her face. "But you have ouchies everywhere."

"It's nothing," she said quickly. She grabbed Becky and held them both for a long time. She started to cry but the kids didn't move. I kneeled down behind her then wrapped my arms around all three of them, rocking them gently. We just listened to Elisa cry.

"Mommy, why are you crying?" Becky asked.

"Your mother is tired and needs a nap," I said quickly.

"Oh," she said. "I hate naps."

"Now you know why she's crying," I said with a smile.

Becky patted her hair. "It's okay, Mommy. They aren't that bad."

Elisa sniffed. "I know, honey."

"Come on. I need to put Mommy to bed," I said.

"Uncle Jared, you're back?" Tommy asked.

"Yeah," I answered.

"Why are you here sometimes but not all the time?" Becky asked.

I didn't know what to say. I picked up Elisa and carried her in my arms. I walked down the hall and entered the bedroom. I laid her on the bed then started to remove her clothes. They were filthy, and I tossed them on the floor. I wasn't attracted to her naked body like I normally was. I was too disturbed and upset to feel anything but pain.

I walked into the bathroom and got the shower running then returned to her. She was sitting up with her arms crossed over her chest.

"Come on. Let's get you in the shower."

She was mute.

I grabbed her hand and pulled her to stand. "Come on. It'll feel good."

"Okay," she whispered.

I walked her into the bathroom. Before she opened the door to the shower, she looked at me. "Get in with me. I don't want to be alone."

"Okay."

She seemed surprised by my immediate agreement.

I stripped off my clothes then I followed her inside the shower. I guided her under the water and started to shampoo her hair, massaging her scalp at the same time. She rested her hands on my chest and closed her eyes. Then I scrubbed her body with soap, rubbing her muscles with my fingertips. When I was finished, she did the same to me. I kept my hands on her waist while she touched me, making sure she didn't fall. When she was done, she wrapped her arms around my neck and just held me. I wrapped my arms around her and let the water fall on us. We didn't say anything but nothing needed to be said. She was still frightened of everything that just happened. She couldn't stand the silence and she couldn't stand to be alone.

When our skin became pruned, I turned off the water then grabbed a towel, drying her skin and tasseling her hair. She closed her eyes and moaned. When she was dry, I wiped myself off. She stared at me but her usual hunger was absent. I wondered if she lost her attraction to me or she was just too confused.

We went back into the bedroom and she crawled under the sheet.

"Please sleep with me," she begged.

"Of course." I moved beside her then wrapped my arms around her.

"I need you to do something for me."

"Anything, Ellie."

"I want you to get me a gun."

The request made me flinch. "You don't need one."

"Please."

"Nothing is going to happen to you, okay? I'm here. I will never let anything happen to you. I promise."

"But you aren't here anymore," she whispered.

I sighed. "I am now."

"But you'll leave tomorrow or the next day. Please do this for me. The man has my address and my keys."

"Ethan changed the locks."

"That still doesn't make me feel better."

"He would have to get through me and Ethan, who already has a gun, to get to you. Those are slim odds."

"My babies."

I grabbed her face. "Ellie, you are safe with me. I will give my life to protect all of you. Please go to sleep. I won't sleep if you want. I'll stay awake and listen to the house."

"No, you don't need to do that."

"Then go to sleep."

She sighed. "Please get me something, Jared."

"I'll get you a tazer and pepper spray."

"I need something stronger than that."

"You have me."

"Do I?"

I climbed on top of her. "I want you for the rest of my life, Ellie."

Her eyes softened as she stared at me. "What about everything I did to you?"

"Forget about it. I was being stupid. I forgive you. Now please be mine."

She started to cry. "You want to be with me?"

"More than anything. I can't be away from you anymore. I have to be with you for always. I have to know you're safe. What's the point in trying to move on when I only want one person? That will never change, baby."

"I'm so happy—as happy as I can be at the moment."

I kissed her forehead. "Just don't hurt me again."

"I won't. I promise."

"I believe you."

She sighed deeply.

"And I'll get a gun and put it in the nightstand, but I don't want you to touch it."

"Thank you."

"Okay. I'll get one tomorrow."

"Will you move in with us?"

I rubbed my nose against hers. "Are you asking me?"

"No. I'm begging."

"Yes. I would love to live with you."

"Thank you."

"You don't need to thank me. I'm not doing you a favor. I love you."

"I love you too, Jared."

"Now go to sleep. I'll protect you."

"I don't want to sleep," she said as she ran her hands up my chest.

"No. I don't want to hurt you."

"Please? You won't hurt me. It will have the opposite effect."

"I can't. I will when you're feeling better."

"I won't feel better until you make love to me," she said as she gripped my back. "Please. I feel safe, happy, and whole when I'm with you. I know you won't sleep with me unless you want to stay with me forever. Please."

"I do want to stay with you forever."

"Then make love to me." She wrapped her legs around my waist. "Don't make me beg."

"I like it when you beg," I said with a smile.

"Please, babe. Please."

"It has to be gentle."

"That fine," she said happily.

"And let me know if it hurts."

"Come on."

I leaned over her then pressed my forehead against hers. I wrapped my arm around her upper thigh then held it back while I moved in front of her. She ran her hands through my hair then down my back. With my other hand, I rubbed her clitoris gently. I knew she wanted to make love, but I also understood that her mind was thinking of other things.

She gripped my back as she felt me.

I pressed my lips against hers and kissed her gently. My heart throbbed as I felt her embrace. I had never loved anyone in the way that I loved her. It was special and unique. She was the only woman who had my heart—the only one who ever would. "I'm so sorry," I whispered.

"Stop."

"I missed you so much," I said in between kisses.

"I missed you too, Jared. You have no idea how much."

"Yes, I do."

"I'm sorry about everything."

"You are forgiven." I rubbed her harder until her legs were shaking. I knew she wasn't thinking about the hospital, the bruises covering her body, or the night she was mugged. She was just thinking about me—only me.

I inserted myself within her in one fluid motion.

"Jared," she said with a gasp. "I miss this."

"I miss this too," I said as I moved inside her. She was soaked like she normally was. She was tight and warm. With every thrust, I felt my body shake. She was the best sex I've ever had. We weren't kinky but our lovemaking was perfect. It didn't bother me that we didn't fuck. I loved staring into her eyes while I moved within her. I saw the same love in her gaze that I knew was in my own.

She grabbed my lower back and guided me inside her. "Harder."

I increased the pace. I started off slower than normal so I wouldn't hurt her. "How's that?"

"Oh."

"There's nothing I enjoy more than making love to you."

She was losing control. I had her where I wanted her. "Yeah."

I moved quicker. "Come on."

She scratched my back. "Oh god, Jared. Jared, Jared."

"Ellie."

Her cries turned to quiet moans. "Jared, Jared."

"My turn," I said as I moved in her. "Make me come, baby."

She gripped my shoulders and rocked me from below, sheathing my cock repeatedly. "I want you for the rest of my life, Jared. I don't want to live without you."

I thrust into her. "Ellie, don't ever leave me."

"Never."

"Yeah."

"I can feel myself coming again," she said as she gripped me again. "Please don't come. Not yet."

I thrust into her hard. "I'm going to come with you. I can't hold on much longer." I pinned her legs farther back, pushing as far as I could go. "Oh god."

She breathed into my mouth. "I'm coming. God, I'm coming."

I felt myself explode inside her I continued to move into her as hard as I could to make her orgasm last while I felt myself shoot deep insider her. Releasing myself was such a turn on. I loved not using condoms, just feeling her wet pussy against my cock.

She kissed me hard as she finished and I darted my tongue in her mouth.

"God, Jared."

"Yeah."

She rubbed my back. "You're so good at that."

"Thanks," I said with a smile. "But I'm only that good because you're so damn fine."

She smiled. "I think there's more to it than that."

"Is it because I'm madly in love with you?"

"That's more likely."

I rubbed my nose against hers. "I love you so much."

"I love you too."

"I'm not going anywhere unless you give me a reason to."

"I won't."

"Promise me."

"I promise."

"Okay." I pulled out of her then lay beside her. I cupped her cheek and stared into her face.

"Can I ask you something?"

"Anything, beautiful."

"Have you had sex with a lot of women?"

I was not expecting that question. "Why are you asking?"

"You just seem really experienced."

"More than most—not a lot." I stared at her expression. It didn't change. "Does that change anything?"

"No. I was just curious."

"Okay. Can I ask you the same question?"

"Just you and my hu—Tom."

I didn't say anything.

She snuggled next to me and closed her eyes.

"Good night," I whispered.

She was already asleep.

# 20

I made Elisa stay on bed rest even though she didn't want to. I woke up early and made the kids breakfast then took them to the park for a few hours before I came home and bathed them. Before I left, I placed a stack of books on her bedside with an assortment of movies to watch so she wouldn't be bored. I knew she needed to heal from the emotional trauma as well as the physical pain, so she needed to be away from the kids for a while. I didn't mind. I loved spending time with them.

I prepared lunch and brought it into her room. When I walked inside, she was asleep, much to my delight. I brought the tray back in the kitchen and saved it for later. The kids played with their blocks while they watched cartoons. I read a book on the couch while I watched them.

When Ethan came home, he removed his tie and hung it on the rack. "When are you going back to work?"

I looked at the kids. "Soon. I wanted to wait until Elisa gets over her cold."

Ethan glanced at the kids then returned his look to me. He moved to the couch beside me so we could whisper.

Nothing had been the same since he punched me in that coffee shop. That was last straw for me. I had put up with Ethan's bullshit too many times. I was sick of it. Sadie hadn't talked to me about the letter but I hadn't given her the opportunity. I avoided her, which was difficult since we were all in the same house.

Ethan looked at me. "What's going on?"

"What do you mean?"

"You and Elisa?"

I put the book down. "I want to be in this relationship. She's forgiven and I trust her. I just asked her not to lie to me again and not to hurt me."

"You mean that?"

"Of course I do."

"So you're serious about her?"

I glared at him. "I've been serious since the first day. Maybe you should ask your sister that question."

He sighed. "I'm sorry. I didn't mean to come off that way."

"Well, you did."

"I take it back. You're right, Jared. I've been an ass to you since the beginning. And I really mean it. I'm sorry."

"Okay."

"Do you accept my apology?"

"Yeah."

"It doesn't sound like it."

"I forgive you but I'm still resentful toward you. Hopefully it goes away soon."

He looked away. "Are you living here now?"

I nodded. "She asked me to move in."

"Are you going to marry her?"

"As soon as she's ready."

"It's getting cramped in here."

"Are you asking me to leave?"

He laughed. "No. Not at all. I meant something else."

"What?"

"Well, Sadie and I are getting married, and if you are here to stay then she, Koku, and I would like to get our own place—have our own space."

"You should. I think I can handle it."

"But I don't want to move out unless I know for certain that you're saying together."

"We are. I won't hurt her and she won't hurt me."

"I would still like to wait awhile. I'll ask Elisa to tell me when she's ready for that."

"Will you tell me?"

"Yeah. I'm assuming that would also mean she's ready to get married."

"Probably."

"So I'll definitely let you know."

"Thank you."

"Yeah."

We were quiet for a moment.

"I need your help with something," I said.

"What?"

"I need to get a gun but I don't know much about them. Can you help me decide?"

"Only if you take shooting classes and gun safety curriculum."

"Of course."

"Then yes, I'll help you."

"I want to teach Elisa too."

"Don't bother. I went through the same thing with her. She won't touch a gun."

"But it might help her sleep at night if she knows she can defend herself." I grabbed the book and rubbed my fingertips across the edges. The kids played on the floor without noticing us.

Ethan watched them. "You're good with them."

"Yeah."

"I'm glad."

I nodded.

"So, when are you going to talk to Sadie?"

"I don't know."

"She cried the entire time you were gone. That letter broke her heart."

"Well, she broke mine."

"Talk to her—please."

"I will when I'm ready."

He stared at me. "I don't like it when my fiancée is upset. You better talk to her soon."

"It's our relationship—butt out of it."

"And she's my girl—don't make her cry."

I shook my head and ignored him.

"You have no idea how pissed she was at me every time I snapped at you. She always defended you, Jared. I just have too much of a temper when it comes to my sister's well-being. I'm the same way with Sadie. But she did tell me off for it."

"She did?"

"Yeah. You only saw the surface. She understood why I was upset but she said I was never allowed to hit you. If I did, she would leave me."

"Then why is she still around?"

He was quiet for a moment. "Because I haven't told her."

I stared at him for a moment. "Are you going to?"

"I don't want to. She said she would leave me. I think she meant it. But when I saw you with that whore—"

"Friend."

"I couldn't stop myself. You just broke my sister's heart. I—I snapped."

"What did she say about your bloody lip?"

"I told her you punched me."

"And was she mad?"

"No. She favors you, Jared."

That surprised me. Perhaps I got all of this wrong. "I won't tell her if you don't."

He raised an eyebrow. "Really?"

I nodded. "I don't want you to break up because of that."

"Thanks," he said quietly.

"Besides, it did look like I was being a huge jackass."

He laughed. "I'm glad you realize it."

"But I didn't sleep with her—or anyone."

"I believe you."

My phone vibrated in my pocket and I pulled it out. Elisa texted me. "My baby needs lunch."

He laughed. "Don't keep her waiting."

I went into the kitchen and reheated the soup and pulled the sandwich from the fridge. I carried it into her room and placed it on the bed. "How are you feeling?"

She smiled at me. "Good."

I noticed the open book on the bed. "What are you reading?"

"*Only For You.*"

"Any good?"

"I think so."

"You hungry?"

"Yes."

I scooted the tray closer to her.

"Babe, I can eat in the kitchen at the table."

"No. Lean back."

She sighed and leaned against the pillows. "I appreciate it but I'm fine."

I grabbed her face and kissed her. She melted at my touch. "Shut up and start eating this wonderful lunch I made you."

She smiled at me. "Okay."

She ate her soup while I watched her. I felt awkward just staring at her like an obsessive stalker so I looked away.

"What did you do today?"

"I took the kids to the park."

"You bathed them, right?"

"Oh, yeah. Tommy decided it would be fun to dig for earthworms."

"Yuck."

"And Becky thought it would be fun to eat the worms."

"Oh my god."

"Your kids are so classy."

She laughed. "My kids are going to grow up to be white trash, aren't they?"

"It seems pre-ordained."

She sighed. "They are something else…"

"I like them. I think they are adorable."

"I'm glad one of us thinks so."

I laughed. "Isn't it nice having a break from them?"

"I guess," she said. "But I do miss them."

"They don't miss you."

"I'm not surprised. I would never let them dig in the dirt like homeless people."

"And then I took them to McDonalds."

"You did not!"

I nodded.

"Please tell me they washed their hands."

"Of course. I admit that I'm new at this, but I'm not completely handicapped."

"Well, you wouldn't know that it's unacceptable to take them for fast food."

"Why?"

"Because I cook for them. I don't let them eat garbage."

"Well, it's too late."

"They are going to have the shits."

"I'll let you take care of that," I said as I patted her leg.

She rolled her eyes. "So much for having bed rest."

When she was done with her tray, I moved it out of the way. "Is there anything else I can get you, Ellie?"

She pulled the covers down and revealed her legs. She was just wearing her panties and one of my shirts. "Yes."

I stared at her.

"I didn't get my morning sex."

"I want you to get better."

"It didn't hurt last night so it won't hurt today."

"I still want you to rest."

"Shut up and fuck me."

I moaned. "You can't talk to me like that."

"Fuck me, Jared. Take off your pants and do it."

My skin prickled. "It's the middle of the day. Someone will hear us or wonder where we are."

"Then make it quick. Consider it a challenge."

I narrowed my eyes at her. "No."

She sat up and turned over, showing me her ass. "Come on," she said as she took off her shirt then removed her thong. She started to rub her clit. "I'm starting without you," she said with a moan.

My eyes widened. I had never seen her act so vulgar with me. I took that as a good sign. I unbuttoned my pants and pulled them down. "Slow down, baby. I'm coming.

She continued to touch herself. "Come on, baby."

I didn't even take off my shirt. I just pressed against her backside and slid inside. The ride was smooth and wet. I moaned. "Fuck yeah."

"Jared."

"Be quiet, Ellie."

"That's so hard when your cock feels this great."

I moaned and pushed her hand away. "Allow me." I rubbed her hard while I thrust into her.

She gripped the sheets as I slammed into her, pushing against me with every move.

I moved my lips to her ear. "This is gonna be quick, Ellie. I'm going to make you come now."

She pushed into me harder. I thrust upward and rubbed the sensitive flesh of her inside to make her shake. When she started to breathe loudly, I knew I found the right spot. I concentrated and fucked her as hard as I could. I knew she was coming when she reached behind me and gripped my ass. The feel of her nails in my skin made my restraint disappear. I started coming inside her.

"I love coming inside you," I whispered. "I love it so fucking much."

"I love it too."

When I was done, I stayed inside of her for moment. I rubber her back and shoulders then pulled out. "Did I hurt you, Ellie?"

"No. Definitely not."

I kissed her forehead. "Good."

I pulled on my pants and adjusted myself. When I looked at the nightstand, I noticed something was missing. "Where's the picture?"

She lay down and looked at me but didn't say anything.

I walked over to the table and looked at the empty surface. "Why did you move it?"

She crossed her arms over chest. "You live here now."

"I made it clear from the beginning that I'm not trying to replace him or make you forget about him. Please put it back."

"No."

"Why?"

"I'm ready to move on, Jared. I don't need that picture anymore."

"Please don't move it because of me. I never want you to change how you feel for your husband. I'm fine with sharing your heart. I've always been fine with it."

"I want to have pictures of him around the house for me and the kids, but it doesn't need to be in our room. I need to make new memories with you."

I stared at her. "Are you sure? I really don't mind."

"You're my life now, Jared. I know Tom would want that. If it can't be him, I know he would want it to be you."

I felt my heart tug in my chest. "I don't know what to say."

"Tell me you love me."

"I love you with my whole heart."

"That's all that needs to be said."

I nodded. "Okay."

She held out her hand to me and I took it. "So, can I go in the living room now? I miss my babies."

"How are you feeling?"

"Fine."

I stared into her eyes and searched for her emotions. "It's okay if you aren't fine, Ellie. You shouldn't be fine." I averted my gaze. I felt pathetic when I looked at her. I was supposed to protect her but I didn't. I was a piece of shit.

"Please don't do that."

"What?"

"Blame yourself."

"Then don't act like you're okay when you aren't."

She sighed. "You're right. I'm not. I'm scared."

"Don't be scared. I won't fail you again, Ellie. You and the kids are safe. You aren't allowed to go anywhere alone and I'll be home every night. You are safe, you are protected."

"I don't want anything to happen to you either."

"It won't. Don't worry about me."

She nodded.

"We'll get past this together, okay?"

"Okay."

I stood up and pulled the covers over her. "Get some rest."

She sighed. "I miss you."

"I'm just down the hall."

"It's not close enough."

"Baby, it will never be close enough."

# 21

Ethan and I went out and purchased my first gun. I filled out the license for it and bought a safety manual. Then we went to the shooting range. I had never fired a weapon and I was glad that Ethan insisted I learn how. I couldn't shoot a bullet through a wall, I had such terrible aim. After a few hours, I was able to hit moving targets and control the bite of the gun.

When we were done, Ethan showed me how to pull the gun apart and put it back together. I copied him until he was satisfied. Then he showed me the safety features and how to use it.

"Don't ever take off the safety unless you're going to use it," he said. "And put this somewhere the kids can't find it."

"Where's yours?"

"In the nightstand, but I keep my bedroom door locked when I'm not home."

I nodded. "I'll get a lock for my drawer just in case."

"You better."

When we were done, we drove back home.

Ethan sniffed the air then looked at me. "Why do you stink? Did the kids make a mess this morning?"

I smelled my shirt. "No. Elisa threw up this morning. I helped her back to bed then took care of it."

"Is she okay?"

"Yeah. She's still stressed out about what happened. I've been making her rest but she still has minor panic attacks. I hope they go away soon. It will take some time."

He nodded. "Yeah, it will."

When we got home, Sadie was in the living room with Koku sitting on her lap. The kids were lying on the couch watching television. I had the gun in my jacket pocket and I kept it hidden from the kids.

Sadie and I still hadn't spoken in private. I could tell by the look in her eyes that she wanted to soon. She looked Ethan. "We need to get a Christmas tree soon. We're running out of time."

"I know," Ethan said. "Let's go now."

"Actually, I wanted to take Elisa," I said.

"Well, ask her, then," Ethan said.

"I'll see." I walked into our bedroom and Elisa was reading on her kindle. "Hey."

"Hey," she said with a smile.

I took the gun from my pocket, checked the safety, then placed it in my nightstand.

Her eyes widened when she watched me. "So you got one?"

"Ethan and I had target practice for a while. Now I know what I'm doing with it."

"Thank you."

"I can teach you."

"No," she said quickly.

I sat beside her on the bed. "You wanna get a Christmas tree with us?"

Her eyes lit up. "I would love to."

"You think you're up for it?"

"I've been ready for it."

"You threw up this morning."

"Well, you cooked breakfast."

"So you're blaming that on me?"

"Yep. I'm desperate. I really want to get a Christmas tree."

"Then get dressed."

She clapped her hands together. "Okay."

When she walked in the closet, my phone rang. It was Layla.

"Hey," I said when I answered.

"Hey. Sorry to call so late."

I looked at the time. It was three in the afternoon. "It's only three."

"Aren't you in London?"

"Oh, no. Actually, I came back a few days ago."

"What? I don't understand." She sounded hurt.

"It's a long story but basically I had to come home, and Elisa and I got back together."

She was quiet for a moment. "Well, thanks for telling me," she snapped. "I went all the way to London for you and you don't have the time or decency to tell me something important like that?"

I felt like a total asshole. "I'm sorry."

"I did everything to help you and then you just treat me like shit? Now I know how you felt last week."

"I said I was sorry. I didn't mean to hurt you."

"I thought you were different. Fuck off." She hung up. I heard the line go dead.

I sighed then hung up.

"She was in London with you?"

222

I looked at Elisa. "Uh, yeah."

Her eyes coated with tears when she looked at me.

"I didn't sleep with her," I said quickly. "Nothing happened between us. She just helped me move."

"She sounds like she's in love with you."

I didn't respond. I didn't know what to say.

"I don't want you talking to her anymore. I mean it."

I sighed. "Well, that shouldn't be a problem. She hates me."

"I don't want her calling you."

I turned to her and wrapped my arms around her. She was wearing a thick jacket with her waterproof boots. "Ellie, there's only you. It's always been you."

She sighed. "I'm sorry. I didn't mean to get jealous."

I kissed her forehead. "I completely understand your feelings. I did go on a date with her. You're justified in being upset."

"I am?"

I laughed. "Yeah."

"But I do want to apologize to her before I stop talking to her. Is that okay?"

"Didn't you already apologize?"

"In person."

"Can I come?"

"If you really want to. It's not necessary—if you trust me."

"I do trust you."

"It doesn't make a difference to me."

"No. You're right. You can go."

"Thank you. Now let's get that Christmas tree!"

She smiled. "Okay."

She and I returned to the living room and grabbed the kids.

"Ready?" Ethan asked.

"Yes!" Becky and Tommy shouted.

Ethan opened the door and walked out with Sadie trailing behind him. I waited for Elisa to walk through but she didn't. She just stood there with a look of fear plastered on her face. It was the first time she was leaving the house since the incident.

"Actually, I'm not feeling well. You guys have a good time."

I put down Tommy and took Becky from her arms. "Go to Uncle Ethan," I said. They both waddled out the door. I turned back to Elisa. "There's no reason to be scared."

She crossed her arms over chest and didn't meet my gaze.

I grabbed her hand placed it on my bicep. "Do you feel that?"

"What?"

"Ouch," I said with a smile. "How about this?" I placed her hand on my solid chest then brought it to my stomach. "You feel that?"

She smiled. "Yes."

"Please don't worry about something happening. I can take care of you and our kids. Please don't be scared."

She said nothing for a moment. "It's just—hard."

"Ellie, I know." I grabbed her face and kissed her. "But do you trust me?"

"Of course."

"Then don't worry about it. I would never put you in danger."

"But you don't know what's going to happen."

"You're right. I don't. But if danger comes our way, I will do everything I can to protect you guys."

"I know."

"Good. Now let's go."

She took my hand and let me guide her outside. I closed the door and locked it. Ethan and Sadie were waiting for us on the sidewalk with the kids. I wrapped my arm around her and we started our venture down the sidewalk.

Elisa was nervous and quiet, staring at the ground the entire time. I wanted to tell her not to stare at her feet, but since it was her first time out, I decided to leave her alone. I kept her close to me and kissed her cheek often, silently reassuring her.

When we arrived at the tree lot, she started to relax. The kids ran down the aisles, arguing about which tree we should get. Elisa followed them and pointed out the different trees to them. I kept a close eye on her at all times. When I saw a man approach her, I was there before the man could even speak.

"Hello," I said politely. "Can I help you with something?" I wasn't going to let this guy even speak to her. I was tired of perverts bothering her.

The man raised an eyebrow when he looked at me. Elisa stepped away with the kids. "Uh, yes. Is that your son?"

Now I raised an eyebrow. "Yes."

"Well, the kiddo took my keys when I dropped them on the ground."

A small laugh escaped my lips. "Oh. I'll get them for you."

Tommy was making them jingle in his hand.

I took them away. "Don't take stuff without asking for permission first." He started to fake cry. "If you make that noise, you won't get to decorate the tree with us." He shut his mouth and remained quiet. I returned the keys to man. "Sorry about that."

He turned around and walked away.

We finally picked out a tree and Ethan and I carried it while Sadie and Elisa carried the two children. Elisa stayed beside me the whole time. When we got it inside the living room, we placed it in a corner and started to decorate it together. The kids had a small section of the tree close to the floor and it looked like they were shoving all the ornaments into one spot, making it look messy. Elisa smiled as she watched them so I didn't bother to show them the correct way. It was too cute.

When we were done, it looked marvelous. The lights shined bright and the ornaments twinkled from the light of the shining star on top. It was the best Christmas I ever had—at least since I was a kid. I felt like I was part of a family. Sadie and I always spent Christmas with my dad but we never decorated a tree. We didn't even exchange gifts. It didn't really feel like Christmas.

I moved to the couch and pulled Elisa into my lap. "You should dress up as a slutty elf for Christmas this year."

"We'll see," she said with a smile.

Ethan and Sadie sat on the couch with Koku sprawled across their laps. The children sat next to us. I was excited to give Elisa my Christmas present. I really didn't want to wait until Christmas to do it. I was too anxious. There wasn't a doubt in my mind that she would love it.

After we ate dinner, Elisa went into our bedroom because she said she didn't feel well. When I went to check on her, she was throwing up again. I thought she had healed from the incident but she clearly hadn't. She seemed to be fine after she vomited, so she lay in bed. I returned to the living room and sat on the couch.

Ethan and Sadie started whispering to one another for a long time then Sadie stood up and sat next to me on the couch. I knew the moment was here. I couldn't avoid it any longer.

"Jared, can we talk now?"

I leaned back. "There's nothing to say."

"Well, I have plenty to say." She stared at me but I didn't meet her gaze. "You are everything to me, Jared. You are my family. I feel more connected to you than I do to Mom or Dad. I'm sorry that I made it seem like I cared about Ethan more than you, but that isn't the case at all."

"It seemed like it."

"I was angry at Ethan for the way he treated you. We argued about it for a long time."

"You let him walk all over me and treat me like shit while Elisa was the one who broke my heart. You never said a world to Elisa even though you had every right to."

"I know. When I asked why you weren't at her birthday party, she told me you couldn't come. I obviously would have said something if she told me the truth. But I did say something to Ethan—many times. I've always been on your side."

I shook my head but didn't say anything.

She moved closer to me and whispered in my ear. "Do you hate him? Honestly?"

I was mute for a moment. "No."

"Do you want me to leave him?"

"What if I said yes?"

She was quiet for a moment. "It would break my heart and kill me, but I would do it if it meant that our relationship would stay the same. I don't want to lose what we have, Jared."

"You really would if I asked you to?"

"Would you break up with Elisa if I asked you to? If I had a valid reason?"

As much as I loved Elisa, my sister was more important. Of course I would do it. "Yeah."

"Then you know that I'm being honest. Now what do you want me to do? If you want me to end it, then I would prefer to wait until after the holidays—for obvious reasons."

"No. I don't want you to do that."

She breathed a sigh of relief. "Are you sure?"

"Marry him."

Her eyes softened. "That means the world to me."

"He and I talked. He apologized for his behavior."

"I didn't ask him to do that, Jared. You know how stubborn he is."

"I know."

"So, we're okay?"

I kissed her on the forehead. "We're more than okay."

She practically jumped on me as she hugged me tightly. I laughed as I held her to me. I knew how much she loved Ethan. She was more than in love with the guy— obsessed. Even if I did hate Ethan, I wouldn't stop her from marrying him. As long as he treated her right and made her smile like she did every day, then I wouldn't jeopardize that. But it did make me feel better knowing that she would sacrifice that relationship for me.

After a few hours, the kids feel asleep on the couch so I put them to bed in their rooms. Ethan, Sadie, and their dog went into their bedroom and retired for the evening. The house was really cramped but I loved everything about it. I loved hearing the kids wake me up every morning. I love having Ethan and Sadie to help with the children. It was perfect. I was actually sad that Ethan and Sadie would eventually leave and start their own lives together.

When I went into the bedroom, I stripped off my clothes because I wanted to make love like I did every night, but Elisa was already asleep. I listened to her breathing and it sounded like she was awake but she didn't open her eyes. I kissed her neck lightly but she still didn't stir. I assumed she was tired so I just went to sleep instead.

# 22

The next morning, Elisa went into the bathroom and vomited right away. I was starting to get worried. Perhaps there was an internal injury that we didn't consider. When I asked her to go to the doctor, she insisted it was just a bug. I wasn't so sure. I told her if it didn't go away in a few days, she was going—whether she wanted to or not.

For the next few days she acted odd. She wasn't as talkative or animated as she normally was. It seemed like her mind was somewhere else. I asked if I did something wrong but she always insisted that she was just tired.

When we were sitting at the table having lunch, she looked at me. "I'm going out to dinner with my brothers. I want you to come."

I looked at her. "You do?"

"Of course I do, Jared. They want to meet you."

"You told them about me?"

She smiled. "Yes."

That meant the world to me. She would never understand that. The fact that she asked me to move in was already indicative of her commitment to me, but this really made my heart squeeze. I wanted to be completely accepted into her family. It looked like I finally was.

That evening, Sadie and Ethan stayed home with the kids while we walked to the restaurant. Elisa was scared to be out but she didn't comment on it. I held her close to me as we walked down the street. I didn't think she would ever move on from what happened. It was understandable.

Her husband had passed away and she almost—I didn't like to think about it.

When we walked inside, I spotted her brothers immediately. They looked like Ethan.

"Hello, I'm Jared," I said as I extended my hand. The man took it. He was bigger than Ethan but with the same blue eyes.

"Kyle," he said with a nod.

I turned to the second brother. "Hello." I shook his hand.

"Scott," he answered.

I pulled out Elisa's chair and helped her sit down before I took my seat next to her. They both seemed to notice my actions because they slightly nodded their heads in approval. At least the night was starting well. I hoped they wouldn't be as confrontational as Ethan was, or worse.

Kyle looked at me. "Ethan said you're a good guy."

"He did?" I blurted.

He laughed. "Was he wrong?"

"No," I said quickly. "He's just threatening me all the time so I can never be sure."

Scott rolled his eyes. "Ethan acts like a tough guy but he's a big pussy who loves pussy."

"Is your sister going to marry him?" Kyle asked.

"Yep," I answered.

"Tell her to get out while she can," Scott said.

I smiled. "Well, that makes me feel reassured," I said sarcastically.

Kyle laughed. "We're just joking. Ethan's not that bad."

"Another golden compliment," I said.

Scott took a drink of his water. "He used to be a disgusting pig but when he met Sadie, he changed. I didn't believe it until I actually saw it. He's being serious."

"I think so too," I answered.

Elisa placed her hand on my thigh. "Jared is a wonderful with the kids. They love him."

"Is that so?" Kyle said. "Good, because Ethan has been playing Mrs. Doubtfire for too long."

Scott laughed. "He actually started to grow breasts at one point."

"Stop teasing him," Elisa said. "Ethan is a wonderful man and I'm so grateful to have him in my life."

Kyle nodded. "Ethan is a badass—don't tell him I said that."

"What do you do for a living?" Scott asked.

"I work on Wall Street with Ethan," I answered.

He nodded his head in approval. "How much money do you make?"

"Scott!" Elisa yelled.

"What? How am I supposed to know if he can take care of you if I don't know how much dough he has?"

"It's okay," I said quickly. "But if Ethan can take of Elisa and the kids, then logically I can as well."

Kyle nodded. "But what if you're an intern or something? How do we know?"

"I'm a certified financial analyst. I graduated from Harvard."

Kyle whistled. "Oh shit. Step back. He just dropped the Harvard card."

I laughed. "Well, I'm throwing all my chips in. I better win."

Elisa rolled her eyes. "Jared is one of the greatest men I've ever known and I want to spend the rest of my life with him."

I turned and looked at her, shocked by her public declaration. If she was ready to get married, I would propose right now. We were basically already married anyway.

"Damn, don't pull a Taylor Swift on me," Kyle said. "I don't want to listen to the mushy love shit."

She glared at him. "Maybe you should settle down."

"Nah," Kyle said. "I've got too many cherries to pop."

"You're so disgusting," she said.

Scott shrugged. "At least he's honest about it."

We talked about everything from sports to literature while we ate our dinner. Her brothers were talkative and disruptive like Ethan but I liked them immensely. I could see myself hanging out with them at the courts, the gym, or the bars. Elisa was lucky that she had three men to care for her—four including me.

Before we left the restaurant, they both shook my hand and gave me a nod of approval.

"Thanks for putting up with my sister," Kyle said. "She can be a drama queen."

"Super annoying," Scott said.

"I guess I'm immune," I said.

"Apparently," Kyle said. They both turned around and walked up the street.

I looked at Elisa. "I'm assuming they don't know what happened?"

"No."

"Are you going to tell them?"

"No."

"Why?"

"It'll just hurt them."

I nodded. "Okay." I could understand that.

We walked back home and went inside. The kids were coloring at the table and Ethan and Sadie were wrapping presents in the living room. There were more presents than we could fit under the tree. Most of them were for the kids.

Elisa sat at the table and watched them color then she took her own paper and started to doodle herself. She seemed to be lost in her work so I moved into the living room. She seemed sad and depressed. I knew the incident was weighing heavily on her mind. She seemed to be out of touch for the past few days. We didn't make love nearly as often as we normally did. I wondered if she was in pain and refused to tell me. I was definitely taking her to the doctor the next day. She couldn't argue with me this time.

When it got late, everyone retired to bed. We put the kids to sleep then read to them before we turned off all the lights in the house, checked the locks, and went into the bedroom. Instead of just taking off her clothes like normal, she changed into pajamas and put on a robe. That shit wasn't going to fly.

"Ellie, tell me what's wrong."

She looked startled. "What do you mean?"

"I know you are upset. I can see it everywhere. Are you in pain? We're going to the doctor tomorrow. You don't get a choice in the manner."

"That's unnecessary."

"Like I said, you don't get a choice. We're going—that's final."

She ran her fingers through her hair then sat on the bed. "I need to tell you something."

I felt my heart race. This wasn't going to be good. I could tell that this was going to break my heart. "Uh, okay." I sat beside her on the bed and looked at her.

Tears started to fall down her cheeks. "I don't know how you're going to react. You might be mad or disappointed. I really don't know."

I took a deep breath. "No matter what it is, I'll still love you as much as I do now, Ellie, so please tell me."

She averted her gaze then clutched her hands together. "Jared—I—I'm pregnant."

My heart burst from my chest like an explosion. I replayed her words in my mind over and over. I was shocked. She was on the pill. I wasn't sure how this happened. It was completely unexpected. She just stared at me but said nothing, her hands still held together.

"Are you sure?"

She nodded. "I've checked many times."

I jumped up. "Yes! This is so amazing! I can't believe this."

She almost fell over she was so surprised.

"I'm gonna be a dad—for real!" I clapped my hands together. "This is perfect!"

"What?"

I walked out the door into the hallway. "I'm having a baby! I'm having a baby!"

Ethan opened his bedroom door with his shirt off. "What are you yelling about?"

"We're having a baby. Elisa is pregnant!"

He broke into a smile. "That's awesome!" He hugged me. "Congratulations."

Sadie came to me next and jumped in my arms. "I'm so happy for you."

"I am too," I said as I squeezed her. "So happy." When I pulled away, Elisa was standing beside me. I grabbed her face and kissed her. "This is so wonderful."

She continued to cry. "You aren't—mad?"

"What? Why would I be mad? I don't think I've ever been happier."

She smiled and wiped her tears away. "I'm so relieved."

I picked her up and held her to my chest. "I'm so glad that's why you've been throwing up. I was so worried, Ellie."

"I'm sorry. I was just scared to tell you."

I set her down then pressed my forehead against hers. "How long until it gets here?"

She smiled. "Eight months."

"*Eight months*? That's forever."

"Didn't you take a general biology class at Harvard?" my sister asked with a laugh.

I rolled my eyes. "I just don't want to wait that long. I want my baby now."

"I'm so glad you're excited," Elisa said.

"Excited is an understatement," I said. "Do you know the sex yet?"

Elisa laughed. "No."

Sadie patted my shoulder. "Okay. Calm down. It's still a long road ahead."

I groaned.

Ethan pulled Sadie into the bedroom. "We'll celebrate tomorrow. For now, we need to sleep." He shut the door behind them.

I picked up Elisa then carried her into the bedroom. I closed the door with my foot then laid her on the bed. I ripped off her clothes like a caveman then kissed her stomach, rubbing my hands across the surface. Her stomach was still flat so I couldn't see any noticeable changes in her body. "Thank you for giving this to me."

"You're so sweet, Jared."

I kissed her stomach again. "This is so hot."

"What?"

"A part of me is growing inside you. Soon you're going to gain a bunch of weight and you'll have a hard time walking around. Your ass and tits will get bigger. I'll be able to feel my baby kick inside you. I can talk to it. Everyone will know that you're mine—that I'm the one who knocked you up."

"So you're excited for me to be fat and bitchy?"

"Yes—so excited."

She laughed. "Thank you for being supportive."

"You don't need to thank me. But I feel like I'm more excited than you are."

"I'm very excited," she said with a smile. "I was just scared."

"I love your kids like my own but I'm excited to have one with you—from start to finish."

"I am too."

"And I want another one."

"Let's not get ahead of ourselves here," she said with a laugh.

I took off my clothes then climbed on top of her. My cock had never been harder. "I can't wait to make love to you."

"I don't look any different."

"It changes everything—believe me. And I can't wait for you to get bigger." I separated her legs then inserted myself within her. "I love you, Ellie."

"I love you too."

"Thanks for picking me. You've made me the happiest man in the world today."

"Oh, Jared."

I rocked into her gently. "It's you and me forever, okay?"

"Yes. That's what I want."

"Good."

I pinned her legs back and moved further inside her. The knowledge that she was pregnant with my child was the hottest thing I've ever heard of. "I can't last much longer."

"We just started," she said as she gripped me.

It was too late. I came inside her. "Oh—god." I bucked inside her until I was completely done. "Sorry. I told you it changed everything." I pulled out of her then moved my mouth down to her entrance. I started to kiss her gently and rub her clit with my tongue.

She moaned for me and gripped my hair. I inserted my tongue within her and rubbed her clitoris with my thumb. Within a few seconds, she reached the edge and exploded.

"Jared," she said with a moan. "Jared."

I pulled away and wiped my lips. "I would never leave you hanging, baby."

I moved up the bed then crawled under the covers, pulling her into my arms. "I love you so much, Ellie. This is what I've always wanted."

"I love you too."

I held her while I closed my eyes. We sat together in the darkness. I started to feel my mind drift as the exhaustion took over. I imagined what my baby would look like as the darkness descended. I heard the heating system kick on in the background. The townhouse was old so it had some mechanical issues with it.

"Jared?"

"Hmm?"

"Is the gun in the drawer?"

"Yes."

"Is it loaded?"

"Yes."

"Okay."

# 23

A part of me was nervous that we were having a baby, but I was definitely excited more than anything else. The pregnancy wasn't traditional. I'm not sure how it even happened because she was on birth control. Perhaps she stopped taking it for the days she was in the hospital and that was enough to make her fertile. There was no point in dwelling about it now. It was done. We were having a kid together.

Elisa had recovered from the incident, but I still preferred it if she stayed in bed or on the couch. I was scared that something was going to happen to her or our baby. Since I hadn't gone back to work yet, I took care of the house and the kids as much as possible. I didn't want Elisa to stress about anything.

When she was still asleep one morning, I went into the living room to see Ethan sitting at the table.

"Hey," he said as he read the paper.

"Hi," I said with a little more enthusiasm than I normally would.

He laughed. "Still excited about the baby?"

"I'm gonna be excited for the next eight months." I grabbed some coffee and sat down across from him.

"So, are you going to ask her?"

I knew what he meant. "Yes."

He nodded. "Good."

The calm behavior was a miracle coming from Ethan. I expected him to hold a fist to my face and threaten to kill me if I didn't propose. It seemed like the guy finally trusted me.

"When?" he asked.

"I haven't decided."

"I think she'll say yes."

"I know she will," I said with a smile.

"So, you aren't getting cold feet about all of this?"

"Of course not. Why would I? This is exactly what I wanted."

He shrugged. "It's just a lot to handle. I love Sadie more than anything, but if she told me she was pregnant, I would be freaking out."

I laughed. "I guess I'm a little nervous, but since Elisa has already done this twice, I know she'll know exactly what to do."

"Then you have to go back to work, right?"

"Yeah, I will soon."

"Do you think you can get your job back?"

"Yeah. I can come back whenever I want."

"That's a relief."

"If not, I'll just work somewhere else."

Ethan flipped the page of the newspaper and continued to read.

Elisa walked into the room, lighting it up with her innate shine. I smiled and watched her pour herself a cup of hot water and grab a tea bag. She wasn't far along, but she looked totally different to me. She was even more gorgeous than just a few days ago. I stood up and kissed her on the forehead. "Good morning."

She smiled then kissed me on the lips. "Morning."

I eyed the tea bag. "You shouldn't have caffeine, Ellie."

"It's decaf," she said as she took a drink.

"I guess that's okay."

She rolled her eyes. "I got this, Jared." She took a seat at the table.

"Are you hungry?" I asked.

"No. I always get morning sickness if I eat," she said as she dabbed her tea bag. "I went through the same thing with the other two."

I sat across from her. "I made an appointment with an obstetrician. He's the best in the city."

She looked at me. "Why?"

"I thought you've done this before?"

"I'll be fine, Jared. I don't need to see a doctor."

I narrowed my eyes at her. "Yes, you do. We are going. End of story." My voice came out harsher than I meant it to, but it just slipped out. When it came to the health of her and the baby, I was a little crazy.

Ethan looked uncomfortable. "I'm gonna go check on Sadie." He left the newspaper and his coffee on the table.

I looked at her. "So go get dressed."

"No."

"What did you say to me?"

"Jared, calm down. I don't need to go right now."

"We need a sonogram to make sure everything is okay. Plus, we need recommendations for prenatal vitamins."

She averted her gaze. "Jared, I don't have health insurance."

"You don't get it through Ethan?"

"We have emergency coverage but I can't afford preventative coverage."

I nodded. "Well, that doesn't matter. I'll pay for it."

"Doctor visits and tests cost a fortune, Jared."

"I don't give a shit. We are going."

"No."

I clenched the table with my fingers. "I have money, Elisa. When have I ever given you the impression that I didn't? And this is my baby too. I want you to go to the doctor and get checked out. You can't argue with me."

She met my gaze. "Jared—"

"Please, just do this for me."

Her eyes widened. "You can't argue with me about this. Go get ready—now."

After she stared at me for a moment, anger brewing her in eyes, she finally left the kitchen and went into the bedroom. I felt horrible for yelling at her but she was being infuriating. I didn't give a shit about the cost of the doctor. My baby's health was on the line. And after we got married, her and all the kids would have health insurance.

She came out forty-five minutes later, her lips pressed together in a line and her gaze averted. I knew she was mad at me but I didn't address it. Sadie said she would watch the kids while we went to the doctor, so we left without further discussion. I held Elisa's hand as we walked down the street. Her hand barely squeezed mine.

I got her into the cab then sat beside her. After I gave the address to the driver, I looked at her. "Ellie, come on."

She looked away.

I sighed. "I apologize for yelling at you."

She still said nothing.

"You were being inconsiderate and it was pissing me off."

"Don't ever talk to me like that in front of our kids," she snapped, glaring at me.

I grabbed her hand. "Elisa, I would never do that."

Her eyes softened. "Okay."

"Don't ever worry about the cost. In the end, what's more important? Money or health?"

"I just didn't want to go in yet. Maybe in a month or two when the development stages are more critical. We can get more for our money."

"Like I said, I don't care about money."

She looked straight ahead and fell silent.

When we reached the doctor's office, the nurse ushered us into a room. Elisa lay on the bed and closed her eyes. I stood beside her and ran my fingers through her hair. The tension from the fight seemed to disappear in light of where we were. I could see the happiness of her face. It matched mine.

"Ellie, can I ask you something?"

"Of course, babe."

"How did this happen?"

She shrugged. "Well, I guess I got off schedule when I was in the hospital and we had sex right after that. Once we were back together, I was so happy that I didn't think about it."

"So, you didn't do it...on purpose?"

She shook her head. "I can't believe you would even ask me that."

"I'm sorry," I said quickly. "I'm not accusing you of anything."

"I admit that I tricked you before you left, but I would never do something like that."

"Okay. I'm sorry I even considered it."

"It's okay," she said quietly.

I placed my hand on her stomach. "I'm really excited about this. Even if you had tricked me, I would still be happy."

"You're so sweet, Jared. I was so scared about how you were going to react."

"Are you kidding? I can't wait to be a father. I've always wanted a baby of my own."

"Well, we aren't married so I wasn't sure how you would feel about it."

"That doesn't make a difference to me. It's just a piece of paper, Ellie."

"Do you think your dad will be disappointed?"

I shrugged. "It doesn't matter if he is. I'm still happier than I've ever been. The opinions of other people don't matter. When you stop caring about what other people think, it makes you feel free." I rubbed my hand across her stomach. "And when you believe in something so much, you'll always stand by it forever. No one can take this feeling away." I kissed her stomach then pulled away.

"I love you," she whispered.

"I love you too."

The doctor came in and shook my hand. He was old, frail enough to retire. He started the sonogram machine and placed the lubricated probe against her stomach. When the image formed on the screen, I couldn't decipher anything. It was a blur of black and gray lines.

"That's the heartbeat," the doctor said, pointing to the small movement within the picture.

I stared at it, mesmerized by the beauty of nature. My whole life was in that picture, the child I would love forever. "It's beautiful."

Elisa squeezed my hand.

"Do you know the sex of the baby?"

He shook his head. "Sorry. That won't be determined until the second trimester."

I nodded. "I'm excited to know."

Elisa smiled. "I hope it's a girl. I want another one."

"I would be happy with either one." I looked at the doctor. "So is everything okay?"

"She's perfectly healthy. She doesn't need any special accommodations or treatment. I'll just get you some vitamins."

I breathed a sigh of relief. "Thank you so much."

"Congratulations," he said as he walked out.

Elisa sat up and I helped her to the floor. She pulled down her shirt and hid the pale color of her skin. I wrapped my arms around her, unable to hide my excitement.

The nurse returned with a bag and gave it to Elisa. She placed it in her purse then we walked to the lobby.

"Stay here," I said when I helped her sit down in a chair against the wall.

"Where are you going?" she asked.

"I'll be right back." I walked to the counter until the nurse looked at me. "I would like to pay for the visit today."

"Well, we'll contact your insurance and have them billed."

"My girlfriend doesn't have insurance."

She looked at her computer and pulled up Elisa's name. "I see."

I opened my wallet and handed her the credit card.

"You usually just send a check after you get the bill."

"I don't want her to see it," he whispered. "Can we do this here?"

She nodded. She pulled up the forms then printed them out. When I looked at the number I was astounded by the cost. I didn't think twice about it and handed over my credit card. I hoped Elisa couldn't see what I was doing.

The clerk ran it through the machine then handed it back to me. "Thank you, Mr. Montague."

"Have a good day," I said as I turned away. I walked back to Elisa and helped her to her feet.

"What was that?" she asked.

"They asked me to fill out a survey," I lied.

She stared at me. "Thank you for everything, Jared."

I smiled. "I'll always take care of you."

"I know."

I grabbed her hand and we walked back to the townhouse.

"After the baby is born, I'll start working," she said.

"What? Why?"

"Well, Tommy and Becky will be in school by then. And I don't want Ethan to support me forever. He's got his own life."

"I'll take care of you. I thought I made that clear."

"Well, I want to help out with the bills and stuff. We're a team."

I stopped and looked at her. "And what are we going to do with our baby? Someone needs to take care of it."

"We can hire help."

I shook my head. "We aren't doing that."

"I can't expect you to take care of all of us. I want to help."

"No."

"Jared—"

"I don't want a stranger taking care of my kid," I snapped. "I want it to be you. I want to come home and see you greet me with a smile and kiss. I want you to cook dinner for me and spend the day with our children. I don't want you to work, Elisa."

"But that isn't fair."

"How? That's exactly what I want."

"Well, I'll start working after the baby gets old enough."

"And what about our other kids?"

"Our other kids?"

"I want to have at least one more."

"You want to have four kids?" she asked incredulously.

"Five, if you are willing."

"Jared, kids are expensive."

"Don't ever worry about money. I have plenty of it."

"But I want to be equals."

I sighed. "It would be different if you had a career that you loved and were passionate about, but if you just want a job for money, then no, it's not going to happen."

"I've been taken care of my whole life. I want to be independent."

"Baby, being a full-time mom is a job. You don't get paid, but it's pure work. I'm sure you agree with me."

She didn't say anything.

"And being a homemaker is work too. Please don't feel like you aren't contributing to the family because I work in business and you don't."

She squeezed my hand. "Okay."

"If you want to get a job when the kids are much older, then sure, but we can manage without it."

We walked a few blocks before we crossed the street, approaching the townhouse a few feet down the road. There weren't too many people out. Everyone was in the shopping centers completing last minute Christmas shopping.

I felt Elisa pull away from me. "What are you—"

I stopped when I saw Elisa being held by the throat with a knife. A man wearing all black with a beard held the edge to her throat. I didn't even see him. I had no idea where he came from. My first instinct was to attack him but I knew that was stupid. Elisa started to whimper in his arms, tears falling down her face.

I raised my hands in the air. "I'll give you whatever you want. Please don't hurt her," I begged. I reached into my pockets and threw everything I had: my wallet, keys, sunglasses, phone—everything. I took off my jacket and threw it on the ground. "You can get a few hundred dollars for the jacket. Please let my girlfriend go."

He still held the knife to her throat while he inched toward the pile.

I kept my hands in the air. "Ellie, it's going to be fine. Just stay quiet."

She whimpered again.

The man kicked the goods around before he looked back at me. "Show me your pockets."

I pulled them out then raised my hands in the air. "You got it all. Now let her go—please." I kept my voice steady so Elisa would stay calm. I had never been more scared in my life. I wished the fucker was holding a knife to my throat—not my pregnant girlfriend. When he blinked, I recognized the freckle on his left eyelid. The anger burst through me in a crescendo.

As soon as he glanced down again, I made my move. I sprinted at him and grabbed the arm that held the knife to my girl's throat. I twisted it down and slammed his arm on my thigh, dropping the knife to the ground. I pushed Elisa away. "Run!" I turned back to the man and gave him everything I had. Now that he didn't have a weapon, he was scared. I punched him in the mouth, then the gut, and then the groin quicker than he could think. I moved so fast that I could barely see what I was doing.

When he kneeled down, he reached for the knife, but I kicked it away then kicked him in the head before pinning him to the ground and pushing his face against the frozen concrete.

"Elisa, grab the phone and call the cops."

With shaky hands, she picked it up and made the call. I didn't take my eyes off the attacker. He made sudden attempts to free himself when he used all of his energy, but I used my weight to keep him down. I wasn't letting him get away.

Elisa stayed on the phone while we waited for help. She was crying the entire time. I wanted to comfort her but I couldn't. I had to concentrate on that motherfucker so he wouldn't escape.

When cops pulled up, they grabbed the guy and handcuffed him. I immediately rushed to Elisa and held her to my chest. "You okay?"

She nodded but didn't speak, crying into my chest.

The cops questioned me while I held her. I told them everything that happened. "It's the same man that assaulted Elisa before."

"How do you know that?" the officer asked.

"He has the freckle on his eyelid. Elisa identified him."

The cop looked at her. "Is that true?"

She nodded.

"Thank you. We'll investigate it."

"Thank you," I said.

They climbed into their vehicles then drove away. Elisa was completely immobile so I carried her home. When we walked inside, we avoided the kids and went to the bedroom. Ethan and Sadie followed us and left the children in the living room.

Ethan opened the door. "Is everything okay?"

I held Elisa and rocked her back and forth. "Shut the door."

They came inside then stepped toward us. I told them the whole story.

"Oh my god," Sadie said as tears sprang to her eyes.

Ethan was silent, speechless.

"But you caught him?" Sadie asked.

I nodded. "The cop said they'll investigate it and determine if it is the same guy. I'm a hundred percent sure it is."

"Did she get hurt?" Ethan asked.

"No. He didn't hurt her."

Elisa sat up and pressed her forehead against mine. "You saved me."

"I'll always save you."

"That was risky. You shouldn't have done that," Ethan said.

I stared at him. "We'll talk about it later."

Elisa looked at me. "What?"

"Nothing," I said.

"Tell me," she whispered.

"I had to do something because I think he was going to kill you."

She gasped. "What?"

"What are the odds that he would be right by our townhouse unless he was looking for you? I think he wanted revenge for pinning him as a suspect."

She covered her mouth and started to cry harder.

I looked at Ethan. "So no, I didn't have a choice."

Ethan ran his fingers through his hair. "Thank you so much. I—I don't know what to say."

"Say nothing," I said. "I would die for Elisa. I would do it again in a heartbeat."

Sadie rubbed Elisa's back. "It's okay, honey."

She clutched me tighter. "I don't know what I would do without you."

"You'll never find out." I looked at Ethan and Sadie. "I got her. We'll talk more tomorrow."

They nodded then left the bedroom, closing the door behind them.

# 24

Elisa was a zombie for the next week. I didn't know what to do to help her. I knew this was something that I couldn't fix. She was traumatized more than any person should ever be. She had been attacked twice in two weeks. That wasn't good for any sane person.

I took care of the legal stuff as much as possible. I testified against the assaulter, Jim Robbins, and recounted every second of the incident. I gave a written statement and was as cooperative as possible. I wanted to see that fucker rot behind bars.

Elisa was asked to come in once to testify and confirm that he was the same attacker from both incidents. It took me a long time to convince her to go, and I still needed Ethan's and Sadie's help to persuade her. I didn't think she was weak. I knew she was severely traumatized. She was so disturbed that we didn't make love for over a week.

She told me how thankful she was that I saved her and how she felt safe with me, but she couldn't forget what happened. It woke her up in the middle of the night, screaming. I knew the recovery process would take a long time.

When Christmas Eve arrived, she was a little better, but I think it was because she was trying to put on a brave front for the kids. She didn't want to ruin the holidays for them. We watched Christmas movies while we drank hot cocoa. We invited my dad over and he immediately loved the kids. He spent more time talking to them than to us.

Sadie told me that my father never even knew I left. She was convinced that I would come back so she never told him the truth. And since my mom never talked to my dad, I knew he would never find out. It worked out pretty well. I'm glad that my sister knew me so well.

"Dad, I have to tell you something," I said.

"What?" he asked as he looked at me. He was playing with Tommy's toys and seemed more interested in doing that.

"Elisa and I are having a baby."

"What?"

I nodded. "It's true." I patted her stomach.

He stood up and clutched his chest. "I'm gonna be a papi?"

I smiled. "Yeah."

There was moisture in his eyes for a moment but he blinked it back. "That's great, son." He hugged me tightly and patted my back. "I'm so happy." He turned to Elisa and hugged her. "This is wonderful."

"We are very excited about it," I said.

"Now I have three grandchildren."

Koku barked.

"I mean four," he said quickly. He looked at Sadie. "And I hope more are on the way."

She smiled. "They'll be here eventually."

My dad hugged me again. "I'm so proud of you, son."

I was not expecting him to say that. If anything, I thought he would be disappointed. "Really?"

"Yeah. You found the woman you love and who loves you. You're a family."

"We're all a family, Dad."

He nodded. "I'm so excited. Have you started planning?"

Elisa looked at me. "We are still discussing everything," she whispered.

We spent the rest of the evening talking about the baby, brainstorming names for boys and girls. I didn't have any in mind. I didn't even care if it was a boy or a girl. I just wanted it to be healthy and happy. If we had a girl, she would be beautiful like Elisa, and that would cause problems with boys. But I guess that is the same issue even if we had a boy.

After my dad left and everyone went to bed, Elisa and I went into our bedroom. I was so thankful that everyone was just as excited for this baby as we were. Even the kids seem excited, though they didn't seem like they really understood what we were saying. We crawled into bed then turned off the lights. I kept the bedroom door open at night so I could hear everything in the house. I preferred to keep it shut but Elisa couldn't sleep unless the door was open. She insisted that I check the gun in the drawer every night as well. Since she was so traumatized, I did whatever I could to make her feel more comfortable. Perhaps in time she wouldn't be so paranoid. I had no right to berate her about living in fear. I had never been held at knifepoint before, nor had I ever been mugged—much less twice. And my spouse didn't pass away because he was killed by a mugger.

She still wasn't in the mood to make love but I didn't push it. I knew it wasn't personal. I would wait until she was ready again. I think she was just too anxious to have sex. Maybe if I tried in the middle of the day it might work better. The sun would still be up. I placed my hand on her stomach while I slept beside her, knowing my baby was deep within her.

The next morning, the kids came screaming into the room.

"Santa came! Santa came!" Becky screamed.

I moaned. "Why did he come so early?"

"No, he came last night, silly," Tommy said. He ran to the bed then climbed on it. "Come on!"

This was another thing I hated about sleeping with the door open. I couldn't sleep naked anymore. "Okay. We're coming."

"No, you aren't," Becky said. "You are just lying there." She grabbed Elisa's hand and started to pull her. "Come on, Mommy."

She sighed then climbed out of bed.

"Yay!" Tommy squealed.

We walked into the living room, rubbing the sleep from our eyes until we gathered around the tree. Ethan and Sadie came in a moment later and sat on the floor. They looked like they wished they could have slept longer.

Elisa went into the kitchen and made a pot of coffee. She handed cups around and we sat together while we watched the kids open their mound of presents. I went a little overboard on the gifts. I bought them way too many presents but I couldn't help it. I was excited to shop for them. I got Tommy a new car set, an action figure set, a car track set, a lego set, a new toy sword, a bag full of dinosaur figurines and other stuff I couldn't even remember. Ethan rivaled my number of gifts. Elisa got them an appropriate number but it didn't seem to matter. The kids just ripped through the paper, squealing in delight as they opened each package.

Elisa got me a picture with the four of us at the park. The gesture touched my heart so much that I felt my eyes become itchy with impending tears. I didn't expect her to get me anything but this said everything that I wanted to hear. She was excited about our baby and our life together. "Thank you so much."

"I love you."

"I love you too." I kissed her then pulled away.

"You got Dad a picture?" Becky asked with a funny face.

Elisa's smile widened. "Yes, I did."

I felt my heart flutter when I listened to Becky. I was glad they considered me to be a father to them, someone who would love them and cherish them, protect them with their life. Elisa's reaction made the moment even more amazing. She seemed genuinely happy.

I'm happy that our kids love you so much," she said.

I nodded.

Ethan got Sadie a white gold bracelet. One side said *Sadie* and the other side said, *Belongs To A Crazy Asshole—Don't Touch.* I assumed it had special meaning to them. He also got her dog a few toys and a huge stack of bones. Koku started wagging his tails happily.

When it was my turn, I grabbed the small red box, the last one under the three, and gave it to Elisa. "Merry Christmas, Ellie."

She smiled at me before she opened it. She stared at the top of the box for a moment before she grabbed a key tied to it and held it up. While she was distracted, I got on one knee in front of her. I heard Sadie gasp as she watched.

Elisa looked at the key then back at me, unsure what it meant.

"I've been saving my money for a long time, and years ago I put a lot of my savings into some stock that did really well. For the longest time, I didn't know what to do with it until I met you. So I bought us a house in Connecticut. It's in a safe neighborhood and it's only a twenty minute train ride from the city. And the schools are the best in the state."

She covered her mouth. "Oh my god."

"Look inside the box."

She picked up the picture. It was a two story house with a porch and a huge front yard. It had a large lawn with a beautiful tree in the middle. She started to cry. "Oh my god. Thank you so much!" She jumped on me and wrapped her arms around me. "It's perfect. I love it! I hate living here, Jared."

"I know, I know."

"I can't believe you did this for me."

"I would do anything for you."

"What about work?"

"It's a short commute."

She pulled away and pressed her forehead against mine.

"You won't have to be afraid anymore."

"You don't understand how much this means to me."

"I do." I reached in my pocket and pulled out the other box. "I forgot something."

She gasped again.

I opened it and showed it to her. "Elisa, will you do me the honor of marrying me, sharing your life with me, having our baby as my wife, letting me love your children like my own, and spending the rest of your days with me?"

"Yes!"

I smiled as I pulled the ring out and slipped it on her finger. "Thank you for making me the happiest man in the world."

She wrapped her arms around me and held me close. "I still can't believe this."

"Believe it."

"I don't deserve you."

"I think you're confused."

"When will the house be ready?"

"It is ready."

"But how did you know I would say yes?"

"There wasn't a doubt, Ellie."

She pressed her face close to mine. "I haven't done anything to deserve this from you."

"Actually, you have."

"What?"

"You agreed to be mine. That's all I ever wanted."

# Epilogue

As soon as we got out of the car, Elisa and the kids ran across the lawn, getting snow everywhere. Becky climbed on the tire swing tied to the tree and Elisa pushed her gently. Tommy threw snow in the air, watching it splash on his face.

I watched them for a moment before I opened the back of the van and started to pull the groceries out. I carried them into the house while they played in the snow, having too much fun to notice me.

Ever since we moved there, Elisa became a completely different person. She was always carefree and happy, excited to be alive. She went for jogs by herself through the neighborhood every morning while I continued to sleep. She went grocery shopping alone and even went out with the neighbor. She wasn't scared anymore and that meant the world to me. Buying this house was the best decision I ever made.

They came through the front door a second later and stripped off their frozen shoes and jackets. I smiled at them and continued to put the groceries in the cabinets. Elisa's stomach was starting to bulge slightly so I limited the number of activities that she did. I stacked the heavier cans while she put the small things into the refrigerator.

The house was big, bigger than we needed since it was just the four of us at the moment, but I knew our family would grow. Eventually there wouldn't be enough room. Elisa grabbed the extra bags and put them in the recycling bin.

"What do you want for dinner?" she asked.

"How about we get a pizza?"

"I can cook."

I shook my head. "Take the night off, baby."

She smiled. "Okay."

The kids went into the living room and started pulling their toys out. The television was on and the cartoons could be heard, loud and clear. She rubbed her stomach while she watched them.

"How are you feeling?" I asked, placing my hand over hers.

"Good."

I stared at her with a hungry expression. I liked her new body. Her breasts were bigger and tender. Her hips were more rounded too. Sometimes I missed having Ethan and Sadie around because they could watch the kids while we snuck away. Those days were over. Only after they were in bed did we get frisky.

"Later," she whispered.

"I'll hold you to that." Fortunately, her sex drive had increased since she became pregnant. She wanted to do it more than I did, surprisingly. When I woke up in the morning, she was already riding me before I could turn off my alarm. Her happiness and smile were infectious. I wondered if it was just the relocation or if it was because we were together. It was probably both.

My only complaint was commuting to work. It wasn't a long ride, but it was still an extra half hour of sleep I lost. When I came home on the train, I hated sitting there for thirty minutes with nothing to do. I never complained to Elisa because it was a sacrifice I was willing to make. It was totally worth it. I loved knowing she wasn't afraid anymore. Sometimes she even left the front door unlocked on accident. I always checked everything before we went to sleep just to make sure. And she told me to get rid of the gun. That was the biggest surprise of all. I returned it to the gun store where I purchased it and only got a fraction of what I paid for it, but I didn't care. I was just glad it was out of the house. The weapon was always kept away from the kids, but I preferred getting rid of it altogether.

Elisa wanted to wait until the baby was born to get married. She said she wanted to be thin and beautiful when she wore her wedding dress. It didn't matter to me when we tied the knot. As long as she agreed to marry me eventually, I was happy.

When the pizza came, Elisa answered the door because I was upstairs. I came back into the living room and started eating with her on the couch. The kids had their own cheese pizza, which was their favorite. We watched a Disney movie so they would settle down and become sleepy. When they closed their eyes, I smiled in victory. I wanted to make love to my fiancée.

Elisa and I carried them upstairs and put them to bed. They were so tired, they didn't wake up when we jolted them. We walked into our bedroom then locked the door behind us. The master bedroom was almost as big as my old apartment. It had a walk-in closet and a private bathroom. Elisa fell in love with it as soon as she saw it. She did a great job decorating it, giving it a feminine touch.

I pulled off my jeans and shirt then washed my face in the sink. I brushed my teeth then flossed like I did every night. When I came back to the bed, Elisa was lying on the surface, wearing black lingerie. The bra pushed her breasts together, making them look even bigger. The thong had glittering rhinestones and fit around her hips tightly. Her stomach bulged slightly, hanging over her waist. It was hard and round, stretched with my baby. I had never seen a sexier woman in my life. Elisa was always commenting on the Victoria Secret models, saying how beautiful they were. I thought they had nothing on Elisa.

I crawled on top her and she ran her hands up my chest, looking into my eyes. There was nothing but love and adoration glowing within them, plus a bout of lust. Her nails dug into my skin, scratching the surface. I liked it when she did this, even if she drew a line of blood. I pressed my lips against her neck and kissed her gently. Her hand glided to the back of my neck and held me closer to her. She wrapped one leg around mine, rubbing her calf against my thigh. They were silky smooth. Her lips opened slightly, moaning quietly for me. Since the kids were just down the hall, our lovemaking always had to be quiet. It's one of the things I hated about having kids, but that was the only thing.

I grabbed the rim of her thong and pulled it down, sliding it down her graceful legs. They were long and toned, exciting me just by looking at them. When she wore shorts, my eyes were always glued to her thighs.

I pressed my lips against the apex of her thighs, kissing her gently. My tongue swirled around her, making her grip my hair so she wouldn't scream. I knew her body better than mine. I knew what she liked and what she didn't like. I came back up then moved further up her body, rubbing my nose against hers. I could tell by her panting that she was ready to feel me inside her. She was growing hungrier by the second, the anticipation killing her.

She trailed her nails down to my waist and pulled me closer to her. Her eyes shined like the lighthouses that called lost boats to shore. Her desire and need was evident in their glow. Her passion for me had increased astronomically once we moved to Connecticut. The relocation finally allowed her to move on and start a new life with me. She loved me so much that it was hard to believe she ever loved anyone else before. She made me feel like I was the only one.

I moved closer to her then she wrapped her legs around my waist, begging me to enter her. I felt my tip press against her. The wetness told me she was more than ready. I slipped inside her and a loud moan escaped her lips. I thrust into her gently, rocking the bed against the wall with quiet tapping. She squeezed me so tight that I almost couldn't breathe. She always clung to me when we made love, scared to let me go.

When her breathing hitched and her nails dug into my skin, I knew her she was coming. Her breaths came out uneven, enjoying the explosion of pleasure that rocked through her. Ever since she became pregnant, she always came quickly. I didn't need to do much to make her explode. She always credited everything to me, but I think her hormones were primarily responsible.

She kissed me when she was done, silently thanking me for pleasing her so well. Every caress of her kiss made me weak. My walls were crumbling and my body couldn't handle the moment any longer. I let a moan escape my lips as I felt myself come inside her. Nothing ever felt so good. Elisa grabbed me tighter as I released myself. When I was finished, I didn't pull away. I continued to look into her eyes, marveling at her beauty. I always hoped my wife would be beautiful but I never expected her to be so extraordinary. She was the light of my life, the sun to the moon. Without her, I was nothing, just a black rock floating in space. I could never tell her how much she meant to me because it couldn't be described. When I saw the same love in her eyes, I knew she was thinking the same thing, that I was someone she couldn't live without. I loved her more than anything and I knew she felt the same way.

# The story continues....

# *Layla*

(Book Three in the Alpha Series)

Available Soon

# About the Author

E. L. Todd was raised in California where she attended California State University, Stanislaus and received her bachelor's degree in biological sciences, then continued onto her master's degree in education. While she considers science to be interesting, her true passion is writing. She works as an assistant editor at Final-Edits.com.

# By E. L. Todd

## Soul Catcher
(Book One of the Soul Saga)

## Soul Binder
(Book Two of the Soul Saga)
Available December 2013

## Only For You
(Book one of the Forever and Always Series)

## Forever and Always
(Book Two of the Forever and Always Series)

## Edge of Love
(Book three of the Forever and Always Series)

## Sadie
(Book One of the Alpha Series)

## Elisa
(Book Two of the Alpha Series)

Made in the USA
Monee, IL
17 August 2023